Why Was He Doing This?

"Do you recall," he said slowly, "our last night on board the cruise ship . . . when we kissed?"

"Yes," she answered reluctantly. "Of course. But you know it was nothing. You shouldn't have . . ."

"Maybe, but I did. *We did.* And it was good, wasn't it?"

"Why are you dragging this up? What's the use of having a post mortem on something that happened months ago?"

"That's a point. Let's try it again, shall we?"

He gave her no chance to say no, and when at last he let her go, he said only, "It's still good, Nicola, isn't it?"

LAUREY BRIGHT
discovered the magic of reading early in life and hopes that her books will bring that same magic to others. Although her interests are varied, including history and ecology, she first began writing stories at sixteen and has never wanted to be anything but a writer.

Dear Reader:

I'd like to take this opportunity to thank you for all your support and encouragement of Silhouette Romances.

Many of you write in regularly, telling us what you like best about Silhouette, which authors are your favorites. This is a tremendous help to us as we strive to publish the best contemporary romances possible.

All the romances from Silhouette Books are for you, so enjoy this book and the many stories to come.

Karen Solem
Editor-in-Chief
Silhouette Books

LAUREY BRIGHT
Long Way From Home

Silhouette *Romance*

Published by Silhouette Books New York

America's Publisher of Contemporary Romance

SILHOUETTE BOOKS
300 E. 42nd St., New York, N.Y. 10017

Copyright © 1985 by Laurey Bright
Cover artwork copyright © 1985 by Mary Guidetti

Distributed by Pocket Books

ISBN: 0-373-08356-4

First Silhouette Books printing April, 1985

10 9 8 7 6 5 4 3 2 1

Map by Ray Lundgren

Silhouette, Silhouette Romance and
colophon are registered trademarks of the publisher.

America's Publisher of Contemporary Romance

Printed in the U.S.A.

Books by Laurey Bright

Silhouette Romance

Long Way from Home #356
Sweet Vengeance #125
Tears of Morning #107

Silhouette Special Edition

Deep Waters #62
Fetters of the Past #213
When Morning Comes #143

Long Way From Home

Chapter One

Jethro Vallance leaned on the stern rail of the cruise ship with his back to the churning wake. He was watching a girl.

He liked the look of her tawny, shoulder-length hair and clear hazel eyes, and she had a becoming tan though they had only been at sea for a short while. Probably a New Zealander, embarked at Auckland, whereas he had boarded at Sydney a few days later. She had caught his casual interest because, like him, she seemed to hold herself aloof.

While a group of young people played a noisy game of deck quoits, she looked on with an occasional smile but no great enthusiasm. When the game finished and the players trooped off to the inside bar, she turned to lean on the side rail and gaze over the vast, inky expanse of the Pacific. The wind blew her hair back, and he noted the regular features of her profile, the delicate curving lines of nose and mouth and chin, the smoothness of a pretty throat. She had a nice figure, too. Studying it, he decided she was probably a few years older than he had first thought—in her mid-twenties, perhaps. Not quite a girl anymore, but a very attractive young woman. Altogether she made a pleasant, graceful and restful picture, with her serene, uninvolved air. Just what the doctor had ordered. He grimaced, laughing at himself, and perhaps he made some sound, for the girl turned her head and for a moment her eyes met his dispassionate grey stare. The hazel eyes darkened, and a flicker of something crossed her face—rejection, perhaps even hostility. She looked away immediately, and within a few seconds she had moved from the rail and walked briskly along the deck to go inside.

Amused at the rather obvious retreat, he wondered if she had thought he was about to "make advances." Nothing, in fact, had been further from his mind. He was on the three-week cruise for the good of his health, and although his doctor had not mentioned women on his list of prohibitions, Jethro didn't intend to indulge in any shipboard affairs. Already he had deftly avoided the indirect approaches of a couple of women who had eyed his tall physique and dark good looks with some speculation. A few months ago he might have been less circumspect, and some part of himself was inclined to jeer at his discretion, but it wasn't in him to betray the loyalty that he owed to Justine, who had only recently agreed to marry him.

He had suggested that she might care to join him on his enforced holiday, but she had said, her dark eyes lustrous and gleaming, "Your doctors told you to avoid excitement. I was under the impression that you found me quite . . . stimulating, darling!"

When she came to see him off, he had teased,

"Aren't you sorry not to be coming with me, to wipe my fevered brow?"

"You haven't got a fevered brow, and if you had, you'd need a nurse, not . . . well, not me."

"You'd look superb in a nurse's uniform."

With an oblique glance, she said, "Is that what turns you on?"

Jethro laughed. "You know what turns me on. Come on, kiss me goodbye; I have to go in a minute."

Justine lifted her face and put her arms round his neck, but after a few moments she pulled her head away and held his with her hands. "There's just one thing," she said. "On this cruise, don't go looking for a substitute, will you?"

"What do you mean?" He half smiled, thinking she was joking.

"I mean," she said, "don't think you can get away with anything just because I'm not there, darling. I'm a very jealous woman."

For a moment he was about to laugh. Then he saw the line of her mouth, the look in her eyes, and was conscious of a small, cold shock. He had never associated Justine with the darker, destructive emotions.

Her hands caressed his hair and linked at the back of his neck. She smiled. "Darling, surely you guessed that I wouldn't stand for you having other women?"

Sudden anger made him raise his own hands, grasping her wrists and firmly bringing them down. "Surely *you* know," he said curtly, "that there won't *be* any other women. I've asked you to marry me. That, as far as I'm concerned, is a pretty exclusive relationship."

"Well." Her brows arched delicately, and her small, red tongue tip moistened her lips. "That's all right then. As long as we understand each other."

He told himself that she had every right to insist on

his fidelity, and that it was unreasonable of him to resent her feeling any need to explicate that right. But the incident rankled, and later the sour taste of disillusion lingered.

Nicola Grey had not been particularly disturbed at finding herself being idly watched by the tall, dark man with the rather inscrutable air. But she had no desire to capture the interest of any man, no matter how handsome and virile he looked. She was reluctant to be paired with anyone, and there were enough shipboard activities between ports of call to keep her happily occupied for the three weeks of the cruise. She didn't mind going shopping on her own at the various islands. They had already called at Nouméa, and her brushed-up school French had got her by quite nicely in the crammed boutique-style shops with their Parisian wares to tempt the tourist. And for each stopover the ship advertised various group trips that would take her to see the sights.

She didn't recall seeing the man who had stared at her before today. He wasn't exactly easy to overlook; there weren't too many like him. His age group was unusual on board, too. Most of the men were either in their early twenties or middle-aged to elderly.

When she saw him again it was that same evening, in one of the bars. She was sitting with her two middle-aged cabin mates, who had invited her to join them for a drink, looked rather surprised when she accepted, and kept hinting that if she wanted to go off and "have a good time with the young ones," they wouldn't be in the least offended. Wondering if they were afraid of spoiling her fun, or planning some of their own that she was blighting, she sipped her cocktail of the day and found her idle gaze briefly arrested by a cool grey one from several tables away. The man nodded, his mouth quirking slightly at the corners, and she gave him a tiny, distant smile of recognition before deliberately turning away.

They berthed next day at Vila, where they had been promised some exciting duty-free shopping. Along the dusty foreshore between the dock and the township numerous stalls were set up, selling clothing, handmade craftware, shells, and toys. Nicola tried to avoid temptation until she had time to discover what else was available, but she couldn't resist inspecting the wares laid out on each stall, and it took her some time to reach the town proper. Other tourists from the ship had taken taxis, and the shops were filled with eager bargain hunters.

She bought an embroidered cotton blouse in a crowded little shop crammed with clothing, fabric lengths, and accessories, then discovered a rack of sarong-style wraparounds in beautiful batik prints. There was a mirror at the end of the shop, and she held one of the garments against herself as she looked in it, then found she couldn't see the hem and stepped back, colliding with someone who caught her arm in a firm grip to steady her. Her shoulder, bared by the sundress she wore, was against a solid male chest, and she felt the warmth of his body heat through a cotton shirt. When he let go, she looked up and found it was the man she had noticed yesterday.

"It's all right," he said in answer to her quick apology, then nodded down at the sarong. "You should buy it," he added casually. "It suits you."

He moved away immediately and left the shop, and she recovered from her surprise, then with an amused smile surveyed herself again in the mirror. He was right, she decided; the sarong did suit her. The material was a light, cool, cream cotton, and the pattern was green shading into browns and golds, complementing the flecked colours of her eyes. She took it to the counter and the assistant wrapped it up.

The ship's entertainment that night was island style, and the passengers were encouraged to dress suitably. There was even a competition for the best-dressed hula girl. The woman who won it had gone the whole hog, with a grass skirt, ankle bands, and flowers in her hair. Nicola didn't enter the competition, but she wore her new sarong dress and a pair of wedge-heeled thongs and hoped she looked more or less in the spirit of things.

After the professional entertainers had completed their very polished act, she wandered into the bar next door, feeling in need of something cool and long. The day had been enjoyable, but walking in the tropical sun had engendered a thirst that seemed to last for a long time, even through dinner and the drinks that went with it.

She asked for a lime and soda, and turned to the sound of a voice that was familiar as the barman took an order from the man who had just come up behind her.

"Hello." He wasn't smiling, but he sounded friendly. "I see you took my advice."

His gaze approved the dress, and she shook her head firmly and said, "Not really. I would have bought it anyway."

He smiled then, and she thought he might be quite devastatingly attractive if he did that often. Just as well, she thought grimly, that she was immune. The barman returned with two glasses and took a note from him and turned away to put it in the till. Nicola, who had been opening her small bag when the conversation distracted her, took out some money and tried to regain the barman's attention, but he was serving someone else.

"I think I've paid for it," the tall man said, picking up his glass.

He hadn't been given any change, and his drink couldn't have cost that much. The barman must have thought that they were together. The voice behind her said, "Don't worry about it. Let's sit down."

He picked up her glass too, so that she had no choice but to follow him to a nearby table and sit in the chair he pulled out for her.

Nicola put the money down on the table and said, "I'm sorry about that. I certainly didn't intend you to pay for my drink."

"Put it away," he said.

"No, please take it."

Patiently he said, "Please put it away. Or are you too terribly liberated?"

"It's not that, only you didn't mean to . . ."

"I don't mind in the least paying for your drink. It's hardly going to break me, anyway. Nonalcoholic, isn't it? Are you an abstainer?"

"Not always. I don't drink a lot, though."

"Wise of you."

He was looking away from her, ignoring the money that still lay on the table. Obviously there was no way he was going to take it. She said as she slid it resignedly back into her purse, "Are *you* too macho to take money from a woman?"

He grinned faintly but seemed to consider the question. "No, I don't think so." In a dry voice he added, "Only . . . someone might get the wrong idea if they saw me doing it, mightn't they?"

She looked up into his teasing grey eyes and said candidly, "I should think you'd be worth more."

A flash of surprise lit his eyes, mingled with laughter. "Thanks," he said in amused tones.

She lifted her drink hastily to her lips. She hadn't meant to say anything so provocative. She hoped he wouldn't get the wrong idea.

"You're travelling alone?" he asked. He was probably just making idle conversation, but she felt she must make it clear she wasn't angling for his attentions. "Yes," she said, "by accident, literally. My friend broke an ankle just before we sailed."

"Hard luck," he commented. "Are you missing . . . your friend?"

"Yes, a bit. But I'm enjoying myself. I've been meeting new people and having a lot of fun."

He looked at her rather keenly. "That wasn't the impression that I got."

Nicola put her drink down rather cautiously. "What do you mean?"

"You may be enjoying yourself, but if you are it's *by* yourself. You've met people . . . one can't help that on a cruise like this. But you haven't been making friends."

"Well, one might not call them friends on a few days' acquaintance," Nicola admitted, slightly nettled by the accuracy of his observation, "but—"

"You aren't in with the crowd," he said. "You've been standing on the outskirts, watching but not joining in."

"How would you know?"

"I've seen you," he shrugged, "because I've been doing the same thing myself. I'm not a joiner, either."

She decided to let that pass. "I'm enjoying myself anyway," she repeated flatly.

He downed his drink in silence, and as she finished hers, beckoned a waiter. "Another?" he asked her.

"Only if I'm paying for this round."

"Unfair. My drinks are more expensive than yours."

"Do you think of that when you're buying for a woman?"

His mouth twitched. "No."

"Well, then." She turned to the waiter and said, "A lime and soda, and whatever the gentleman's having."

"Very independent," he said as the waiter moved away. "And if we're buying each other drinks, it's about time we introduced ourselves, isn't it?"

"Nicola Grey," she said.

"Jethro Vallance."

"Jethro," she said. "It's unusual. Is it biblical?"

"I believe so. Not that my parents were religious, particularly. I guess they just liked it."

"I think I like it, too. It suits you."

He smiled. "Thank you again."

She hadn't meant it as a compliment, exactly. She glanced at him with some suspicion, but his manner was still casually friendly.

They talked, over the second round of drinks. He was in publishing, he said, and she was interested in that because she worked as the senior assistant and fiction buyer in a bookshop in Auckland. The conversation naturally turned to books, and they discussed amicably the merits or otherwise of some recent works. She said regretfully that she didn't think she had heard of the firm he worked for, and he asserted with confidence that she would. It had been a small family business for many years, specialising in minor works on Australian history, but lately it was under a new management and was growing rapidly, improving the books' design, expanding the previously very small fiction list, and employing more staff to actively seek out new writers and entice experienced ones into the house's "stable."

"Are you one of the new editors?" she asked.

"Not an editor. I'm more on the business side," he said. "With overall responsibility for making sure the whole works run smoothly."

"That must be quite a job."

He grimaced. "You'd be right, there. It's the main reason I'm on this cruise."

She looked enquiring, and he laughed deprecatingly. "Overwork," he explained. "So my doctor tells me. I was getting to the stage where I didn't remember things—important things—and I was tired, and overusing stimulants to compensate. Too much drink, too much tobacco, even too much coffee, according to my medical advisor. I went to him looking for some sort of pick-me-up, and he laid it on the line. Reckoned I was looking for a heart attack at forty if I didn't stop smoking, cut back on the alcohol, and take some real time off. So here I am, away from the office, out of reach of the telephone, giving away the demon tobacco, and relaxing like mad to the utmost of my ability. And I'm sorry, I didn't mean to inflict my boring medical history on you."

"I've heard worse. I've an elderly great-aunt who's had every operation in the medical textbooks, and she likes nothing better than giving a blow-by-blow description of the latest one every Christmas. It's become a family tradition. My brother calls it 'Aunt Muriel's soap operation.'"

"Sounds more exciting than Dickens," he commented. "I never did take to *A Christmas Carol*."

"What, not Old Marley's Ghost?" she asked. "I think he's delicious."

"Maybe, but you must admit Tiny Tim is a nauseating child."

"Poor little Tim? What sacrilege! How can you say that?"

"Easily." He grinned. "Dickens was a genius of comedy, but his sentimental passages were the purest bathos."

"The Victorians didn't think so," she objected. "You have to make allowances for the times he wrote in."

"Other writers managed to avoid the slush."

"Name one."

He laughed at the challenge in her tone, and said, "Emily Brontë. A woman without a sentimental bone in her body."

"Do you think so?" She leaned forward, forgetting her drink, and soon they were deep in amicable argument.

It was almost two hours later that he suggested a walk on the deck. For a moment Nicola hesitated, and he grinned and said, "No hands, I promise," lifting and spreading them as he spoke.

Nicola smiled back, fairly sure that she wouldn't need to remind him to keep his hands to himself. They strolled out into the night and shared a pleasant walk before he saw her down to her deck and nodded a casual good-night to her at the foot of the stairs. She hadn't enjoyed herself so much since coming aboard.

Two days later they were ashore again, this time on a small island in the Fiji group, where tourism had hardly gained a toehold and the chief attraction was a visit to a sea-cave where they were treated to a concert by some local singers and dancers, and later an island-style buffet lunch. The ship's passengers who had booked for the tour were transported in several buses, and it wasn't until lunch that she realized Jethro had come along on the trip. He smiled at her, but he seemed to be with a group of people and didn't approach her.

Later that evening she was reading in the ship's

library when he walked in. He nodded to her as she glanced up, then went to one of the writing desks in a corner of the cabin.

Nicola returned to her book. A little later someone else came in and she heard a light, feminine voice saying, "Oh, there you are, Jethro! We were wondering where you'd got to! They're dancing in the big lounge. You're welcome to join us at our table."

"That's very kind, but I really have to get these letters finished before we get to the next port, I'm afraid."

"Oh, well . . . if you change your mind. Rita loves dancing, and she hasn't got a partner so far."

"I'm sure she'll find one."

"Well, see you later then, maybe?"

"Maybe. Thanks for the invitation."

The woman left, and Nicola tried to reconcentrate her attention on the story she was reading. She finished the chapter and closed her book. But as she rose, Jethro turned from the desk and got to his feet, too. "Nicola," he said, "can we talk for a minute?"

"Yes, of course." She waited, and he indicated that she should sit down again. When she did, he sat beside her, half turned toward her and said, "I'm not quite sure how to put this, but—you must have heard the conversation just now."

"Yes," she agreed. "I couldn't really help it."

"Of course not. The thing is, to put it bluntly, Brenda—the woman I was talking to just now—has got it into her head that it would be nice to pair me off with her sister."

Nicola raised her brows slightly in enquiry, wondering what this had to do with her.

"Rita," Jethro continued, "is recently divorced and miserable about it. Personally, I think she's even less inclined to want this kind of matchmaking than I am.

Brenda means well, and her sister doesn't seem able to tell her to mind her own business. I suspect that Rita's off men for a while, and I certainly don't want to be the one trying to pick up the pieces, even if . . . well, I'm committed to a woman back home, anyway, and I don't cheat. I've mentioned that I'm engaged, but it didn't seem to penetrate at all. Either Brenda genuinely believes that what Rita needs is some kind of shipboard affair to get her over the divorce, or she's finding Rita's unhappiness too much to cope with and simply wants someone to take the poor woman off her hands. Either way, I don't fancy being a candidate."

"I don't blame you," Nicola murmured, shifting uncomfortably in her chair. Did he think she was some kind of Agony Aunt? "But . . . why tell me?"

He paused for a moment. "You don't seem interested in pairing off either," he said. "You must have had chances—in fact, it's been obvious to the most casual observer that some of the men on board were interested, but you've brushed them off. I thought possibly you were committed to someone, too . . . ?"

Nicola shook her head, not volunteering any information.

He noted her evasion with a slight narrowing of his eyes, and went on. "Anyway, it occurred to me that—perhaps you wouldn't mind helping me out."

"Helping you out? In what way?"

"We got on rather well last night. I hope I'm not wrong in thinking you enjoyed it as much as I did. I wondered if we might agree to spend some time together, without any strings or any—expectations."

She gave him a guarded look, and he said, "If you're hoping to meet someone, say so and I'll forget this idea, or if you agree, and then do find someone later in the cruise, I'll fade out of the picture. . . ."

"I didn't come on the cruise looking for a holiday

romance," she said sharply. "I just wanted to see the islands and enjoy being pampered and entertained for a bit."

"You must admit that the entertainment could be more fun with a companion, though," he urged. "I'm finding that myself, but I prefer to choose my own company rather than have it thrust on me. As your . . . friend isn't here, and you obviously don't want to be involved with anyone, I thought we might both benefit from a sort of partnership arrangement."

"A platonic partnership?"

"Yes," he agreed. "Exactly."

Nicola thought about it for a minute. "Do you dance?" she asked. "It's the one thing I've been missing out on that I would have liked a partner for."

"I do." He smiled, raising his brows in a silent question.

"Yes," she said, making up her mind. "I think it's a very sound idea."

In the next two weeks she had no reason to regret her decision. As one of a pair she was able to take part in more of the activities provided for the passengers, and yet because of her understanding with Jethro there was no danger of getting into a deeper relationship than she wanted. They entered a Scrabble tournament and won decisively. They went out together in a glass-bottomed boat off one of the islands to spend a day happily exploring the surrounding coral reef, exclaiming at the brightly coloured fish, spotted shells and peculiar sea creatures that abounded among the vivid coral. And they danced nearly every night until the band packed up and the bar closed. Sometimes, when the music was dreamy and the lights low, Jethro would draw her closer to him, and once she caught him looking at her with something like speculation, and was suddenly conscious of the muscular thighs moving against hers, the warm strength of his hand on her waist as he guided her across the tiny dance floor. But she kept a firm hold on her emotions, and when she eased away from him, he grinned and gave her a teasingly sardonic look that suggested she was overreacting. He certainly seemed quite content to stick by their bargain. Unwillingly she had to admit that he was an extremely attractive man and a stimulating companion. They laughed a lot, enjoyed doing things together, and shared some amusement at the candid photographs of them the ship's photographer had snapped, particularly one in which he had caught them looking positively smoochy while dancing. "How did he get *that?*" Nicola exclaimed in disbelief when they found it displayed on the board by the purser's office.

Jethro peered at it and grinned. "I know," he said. "Remember the night when the ship was pitching like mad and the floor wouldn't stay under our feet?"

Yes, she did, and she recalled one enormous heave when she had clutched at him wildly to keep her balance, and everyone else was doing the same, laughing and huddling together. In the photograph she had her eyes shut and his head was bent, a smile on his face, their arms wound about each other tightly in what appeared to be a passionate embrace.

"Do you want a copy for a souvenir?" he asked her.

"No," she said, shaking her head, and then, "Yes, why not?" It would be funny when she showed it to her family and explained what had actually happened.

She insisted on paying her half of the expenses when she and Jethro were together, but he said he wanted to give her the photograph and she gave in without a lot of argument. She didn't ask him whether he was keeping one for himself as well.

The night before the ship berthed again at Sydney, they danced until the small hours, and afterward went out on deck and hung over the rail admiring the stars and listening to the hiss of the ship's wake.

"Enjoyed your cruise?" Jethro asked her.

"Mm. Better than I expected," she said. "It did begin to look as though I was going to miss out on a lot of fun without my friend. Thank you, Jethro."

"Thank *you*," he said. "I feel like a new man, and it's largely due to your blessedly uncomplicated company."

"Well, I hope your recovery is complete and you won't overwork yourself anymore. What was the name of your publishing firm, again?"

"Arcadia Press."

"I'll look out for your books."

He said, "You never did tell me if your friend who was supposed to come with you was male or female."

"Oh, female," she said.

"I thought it might have been a boyfriend."

"No."

She didn't add to the monosyllable, and after a moment he said, "Well, I'm glad we found each other, Nicola. It's been a good holiday. I hope you've enjoyed it as much as I have."

"I'm sure I did." She straightened away from the rail, ready to say good-night. She might get up early to see the ship come through the heads and into the harbour, and Jethro might too, but this was their private good-bye.

She held out her hand, and he put his warm, strong fingers over it, then suddenly bent and kissed her very lightly on the lips. "Good-night, Nicola," he said, "and thank you."

She smiled and moved her fingers tentatively, but his grip had imperceptibly tightened, and he pulled her closer, lifting her hand in his so that it lay trapped between them, his arm coming about her as he kissed her again, properly. His mouth was firmer this time, and her lips opened softly under its gentle pressure, her free hand on his shoulder. She felt an unmistakable stirring of desire, and caught her breath as he deepened the kiss and for a few moments passion flared between them. Then he seemed to check himself and gradually eased the pressure on her mouth, returning to gentleness. When they parted she took a quick breath and avoided his eyes.

He said softly, "Thank you again, Nicola. Goodnight."

She whispered a reply and left him standing at the rail in the darkness.

The kiss had been more than she expected, more than he had too, she rather thought. She was pretty sure it had been a sudden impulse on his part, but she couldn't regret it, and she didn't suppose that he would either. As a kiss it had really been quite terrific, a nice memory to finish her holiday with, and certainly not anything to be upset about.

She was up early, and as the pilot boat guided the ship into the harbour she stood with a small crowd of passengers watching the morning light spread over the indented bays, the tall headlands and the silvery water. Later Jethro came and silently stood beside her. They still had not spoken when the giant white butterfly arches of the Opera House welcomed them to the inner harbour, and the solid metalwork of the famous bridge flung from shore to shore loomed over them.

Then they shook hands as they had not done last night, and smiled in mutual amusement at the incongruity of it, and parted. Jethro was a Sydneysider, and although the cruise itinerary ended here, Nicola was being flown across the Tasman Sea by the shipping company. The last leg of the journey was an anticlimax, but as the plane started the long glide to Mangere airport, she saw the glitter of the Waitemata and the Manukau, twin harbours flanking the city of Auckland, and was glad that she was home.

Chapter Two

She was met by her parents and her younger sister Susan, who asked so many questions about the cruise that Nicola was kept busy answering them until they drew up at the house, a modest bungalow in the pleasant, leafy suburb of Meadowbank. As they helped her get her luggage out of the car, her mother said, "We invited the Lawrences to come round after tea. Jenny's leg's still in plaster, but she gets about with a cane now, and she's dying to find out just what she's missed. Carol's home, by the way."

"Oh, is she?" The Lawrence's elder daughter had gone to live and work in Australia some years ago, and seldom came home, although Mr. and Mrs. Lawrence had holidayed in Sydney last year and stayed with her. "Home to stay?" Nicola asked curiously.

"Well, indefinitely, anyway."

"She doesn't seem to have really made up her mind,"

Susan said. "She says she got sick of Sydney and wanted a change, but I think it's something to do with a man."

A broken romance? Nicola wondered. Poor Carol. A pang of pity mingled with a grief that was more personal made her turn away for a moment to hide her expression.

The visitors arrived soon after Susan and her mother had washed the dishes while Nicola started unpacking. The families had been friendly since the children were quite young, and had each year rented "baches" next door to each other at Piha, a popular west coast beach not far from Auckland.

If Carol was heartbroken she didn't show it. She looked very poised and well groomed in a gold Thai silk blouse and brown skirt, and Nicola remembered that she had been working as a sub-editor for a glossy monthly that specialised in fashion and the latest trends in Sydney life-styles. She certainly looked the part.

Nicola had already distributed small gifts to her own family. She had also bought a batik wraparound skirt for Jenny and a mother-of-pearl dish and a pair of carved bookends for Mr. and Mrs. Lawrence. Carol looked on and briefly admired everything as Nicola handed the presents out, and smilingly shrugged at Nicola's apology for not having one for her. "I've got all the duty-free goods I'm likely to need, thanks," she said. "And of course I don't expect a present from you."

"Susan, show Carol the lovely dress Nicola got for you in Fiji," Mrs. Grey suggested. "I'm sure she'd like to see it."

The dress was produced and admired, and Jenny pounced on the large envelope containing photographs that Nicola had taken with her new camera, the postcards she had collected from the various islands, and a few prints bought from the ship's photographer.

"How about a cup of coffee?" Susan suggested, and went off to the kitchen to make it.

Nicola began passing round photographs of the ship, the lifeboats swinging on their davits, sunbathers by the swimming pool, and a shot of the bow taken from the bridge on the one occasion when she had been privileged, with a group of other eager passengers, to visit it. The photographs went from hand to hand, and she answered questions and retold shipboard incidents. As she started on the second packet, someone said, "Where's that coffee? Susan's missing out on this."

"I'll go and see," Nicola volunteered, jumping up. She was getting tired of talking anyway, and could do with a drink of something. Susan was mopping up a spill with a cloth. "Sorry I've been so long," she said cheerfully. "Had a bit of an accident with the coffee pot. I've had to put a second brew on."

"Clumsy clot," Nicola said with absent affection. "What can I do?"

"Put some sugar in that bowl, and whip up some cream, if you like." Wiping up the last of the coffee, Susan glanced at her sister curiously. "You do look a lot better, Nic. Have you quite got over Robin?"

Nicola, concentrating all her attention on pouring sugar from a paper bag into the silver bowl, said steadily, "Yes, I think I have."

Hesitantly, Susan said in a low voice, "He . . . he's married, you know."

Nicola put down the bag of sugar with a thump on the table. Pain arrowed through her, and her forehead went clammy. "Yes," she said thinly. "I expected that." But expecting it didn't make it any easier, and for a few seconds she was back in the nightmare of two months ago, when Robin had told her that he wanted to break their engagement because he had fallen in love with someone else. They had been in this very room at the time, she recalled, sitting at opposite sides of the small table that the family used for breakfast on weekdays. He had held her hands while he told her, looking flushed and speaking awkwardly, but doggedly determined. "I'm sorry, Nicola, but I can't go through with it," he had told her. "It wouldn't be fair to you or . . . to her."

"But you love me!" she said stupidly, unable to believe what he was saying. They had been so sure of each other, their love growing from a friendship that went back to schooldays. Both of them had dated others, but in the last year they had become close and gradually exclusive, neither of them wanting to see anyone else, until Robin had finally said to her with mock casualness, "We're together such a lot, we might as well get married, don't you think?"

She had agreed instantly, and the wedding was only weeks away when he dropped the bombshell of his involvement with someone else.

"It's different," he said. "I love you, Nicola, of course I do. But with her . . . I'm *in* love, and there's no comparison. It was so quick . . . but I know that she's the one. I'm sorry," he repeated. "I don't want to make you unhappy, but it wouldn't work, feeling the way I do about someone else. I wish I didn't have to hurt you, but maybe some day you'll feel the same way about someone, and then . . . you'll understand."

"I feel that way about you!" she whispered.

He had let go her hands then, as though she had embarrassed him, and she realised that he didn't want to hear any loving words from her. That was when the pain began, the constant ache that never left her. She had taken the cruise, using money she had saved for setting up house with Robin after their marriage, in an effort to dispel the pain, and it was true that the constant round of enjoyment, and the new places and faces, had pushed the memory of hurt and humiliation to the back of her mind. But now the mention of Robin's name, the news of his marriage, the memories of him conjured by her home, where they had spent much of their time together, were rapidly undoing the healing process that had begun. . . .

Susan said, "Are you all right, Nic? I'm sorry, but you were bound to find out sooner or later. I thought, better one of us . . ."

"Yes." Nicola managed a smile. "It's okay, Susan. I'm fine, honestly. Where did you put the cream?"

"Here." Susan handed her the bottle. "I could hit him for what he did to you," she said warmly. "We all liked him so much, and you seemed so right for each other. How could he have just fallen for someone else out of the blue? I'll never understand it."

Neither will I, Nicola thought. He must have been seeing the other girl while he was engaged to her, weighing the attractions of one woman against the other, and finding her—Nicola—wanting. He was the only man she had ever been truly serious about, because her temperament was basically reserved, and although some of her earlier men friends had awakened her to the possibilities of her own sexual nature, she didn't give love easily. When she finally had, it was wholeheartedly, and from then on she had never looked at another man.

She had been completely trusting in her love, would have sworn by Robin's loyalty and integrity. But her judgement had been wrong. She knew nothing about him—nothing, it seemed, about men in general. For if she had been wrong about him, knowing him as intimately as she had, she could be wrong about them all.

When the coffee was ready they carried it into the other room, and Jenny asked a question about one of the photographs. Nicola looked at it and said automatically, "Oh, those are the firewalkers."

Interest sparked, and she found herself telling them about the Fijians walking on hot stones in bare feet and remaining perfectly unharmed. She heard her own voice talking quite calmly and was amazed. She felt like two different people—one who was dwelling on past grief, reliving every painful moment, and the other who could go on acting like someone who had just returned from an enjoyable trip. Even the sofa on which she was sitting next to Mrs. Lawrence brought back memories of Robin, of lazy afternoons when they had sat side by side, his arm about her shoulders, his lips nuzzling at her neck, his hands gently turning her face to meet his kiss. The cruise hadn't really worked at all, she thought, desperately depressed. A couple of hours back home and all she could think about was Robin and what she had lost. She must somehow pull herself together. She couldn't spend her life on a cruise ship. Perhaps she would get used to it, learn to live with the reminders.

Mr. Lawrence suddenly said with heavy humour, as he opened another packet of photographs and took out the prints, "Hello, now, what's all this then, eh?"

Jenny leaned over her father's shoulder and cast a surprised, questioning look at Nicola. Carol, intrigued, held out her hand for the photo, and Nicola caught a glimpse of it and realised it was the snapshot of her and Jethro that he had bought for her. She had been going to make a funny story of it, she remembered, but that was quite beyond her at the moment.

Carol said, "Who is he?"

"Just someone I met on board," Nicola said shortly. "His name's Jethro Vallance."

Carol glanced down again at the photo, her face thoughtful, and her father, smiling broadly said, "More than met, I'd say. You two look pretty friendly."

Nicola said, without thinking, "Yes, we were quite friendly."

"Let's see!" Susan went over to inspect the picture, taking it from Carol.

"*Quite* friendly!" she said derisively. "I should say so!"

She looked at her sister with blatant speculation. Her parents, too, looked pleased and interested and hopeful, as the photograph was passed around. They were all, she realised, sorry for her and patently eager for her to have found someone to replace Robin in her heart, or at least to make her "forget" him. Her family were dear to her, but their sympathy at the time of the broken engagement had been almost more than she could bear. She had wanted to crawl into a hole and hide from the world, while they had felt that getting "out and about" would be good for her, dragging her to parties and social events she didn't want to attend, but went to partly so as not to hurt their feelings when they had gone to the trouble of making the arrangements, and partly because she had a forlorn hope that they were right.

Going on holiday had been a way of getting away from their solicitousness, as well as a retreat from the trauma of Robin's defection itself. But something more was needed. She would leave home, find a flat, and perhaps even her mother, who was inclined to over-protection and had been hurt at the suggestion when she had made it once before, would understand this time.

Jenny had taken the print back and was saying, "Is he as dishy in real life as he looks here?"

"Yes," Nicola said absently, her mind busy, "actually he is."

"Wow!" Jenny gave the photograph her full attention. "Now I really know what I've been missing! Were there many like him?"

Trying to smile, Nicola shook her head. "Jethro's one of a kind," she said, sure it was true.

"What does he do?" Carol asked her.

"He's in publishing."

Susan said, "Where?"

"Sydney," Nicola told her.

"Oh." Susan seemed disconcerted. "Then you won't be seeing him again."

Something clicked into place in Nicola's mind. It was easy, a beautiful, simple, clear solution. She could stop everyone feeling sorry for her, get away from the increasingly claustrophobic atmosphere of her home without offending her mother. . . .

"I may," she said calmly. "As a matter of fact, I'm going to fly over to Sydney again as soon as I can arrange it."

It was so simple, so obvious, and it had come to her in a flash of inspiration. The cruise had taken most of her savings, but she still had enough to pay for the air fare to Sydney.

Her mother gave a shocked exclamation. "Sydney! You've only just got home."

"I know," she said. "Sorry, Mum. I didn't mean to spring it on you like this, but . . ."

"This man must be pretty special?" her father interrupted quietly, his enquiring glance shrewd and concerned.

"Yes," she said. "He . . . he is pretty special." It wasn't a lie, she told herself; Jethro wasn't any ordinary person, though he wasn't special to her in the way her father was implying.

"Why can't he come here?"

"He's busy," she said. "He has a very responsible job . . . in fact, that's why he needed a holiday, the strain was getting to him. He's just had three weeks off for the cruise and he can't afford to take any more time."

"You're not planning to do anything drastic, are you?" her mother asked apprehensively.

Nicola managed a laugh. "No, of course not. I'll find a job in Sydney, and then . . . well, we'll see."

"I don't like it," her mother said.

"But it's so romantic!" Jenny exclaimed.

"Yes, don't be a spoilsport, Mum!" Susan protested. "You can't stop her. She's over twenty-one."

Her father said, "That's true. But I wish you'd think about it, Nicola. A shipboard romance is all very well, but you might find him not the Prince Charming he seemed when you see him again."

"You can't go alone!" her mother wailed. "A young girl, on your own . . ."

Carol laughed. "I was younger, Mrs. Grey, and I survived. I can give you some addresses if you like," she offered to Nicola, "although I expect the boyfriend will look after you."

Nicola would have liked to say that Jethro wasn't her boyfriend, but she didn't know how to put it without arousing suspicion, so she just said "Thanks" instead.

Soon afterward the visitors went home, Mrs. Lawrence saying that Nicola looked tired and they should let her rest, as she must have had a long day.

She was tired, but she didn't sleep. She wondered if she had been quite mad to put herself in such a false position, but the more she thought, the more the solution she had hit on so unexpectedly seemed to be the right one. It gave her a perfect excuse to leave New Zealand with all its painful memories, and although she was uneasy about using Jethro's name, she decided she was being too scrupulous, because he need never know, and if he did, he probably wouldn't mind too much anyway. He might even find it mildly amusing.

She arrived in Sydney on a clear sunny day that didn't match her mood. Perhaps because she had allowed her family to infer that she was to be met by the man she was supposedly flying to in such haste, she unexpectedly felt the loneliness of being in a strange city on her own. At the airport everyone else in the huge, crowded concourse seemed to have friends there, and she found herself already missing the family she had crossed the Tasman to get away from. Telling herself not to be so childish, she found a taxi and asked the driver to take her to a women's hostel.

She was able to secure a small, neatly furnished room, and after freshening up and unpacking the few things she would need immediately, she looked up the first address that Carol had given her. This was Carol's erstwhile flatmate, and it resulted in an invitation to a meal at the flat the following evening. Nicola bought some newspapers and spent the rest of the afternoon poring over the "situations-vacant" columns and making telephone calls, only one of which resulted in a request for an interview the following day.

She was turned down for the job, which was serving in a dress shop, in favour, the owner said, of a girl who had already some experience in boutique work. She bought more papers, and made more phone calls without success.

When she turned up at Carol's former flat that evening, she was cheered by the casual friendliness of Marion Jones and her new flatmate. "I just got a letter from Carol today," Marion told her. "She mentioned you might get in touch, but I don't think she really expected you to. I gather you know someone in Sydney quite well, and she thought he'd probably keep you fairly busy." It wasn't quite a question, but there was lively curiosity in her eyes.

Jethro had by now assumed a mythic quality in Nicola's mind, an invented person who had been the means of her escape from an impossible situation. She hadn't thought of Carol writing to her friends about her supposed reason for being in Australia. Somewhat cautiously, she asked, "What did Carol tell you?"

"Just that you'd met this gorgeous guy on a cruise and were flying over to meet him again. It all sounds dead romantic."

Nicola summoned a smile, saying nothing.

"Oh, well, if you don't want to talk about it . . ." Marion said agreeably.

"Do you mind? I'd really rather not."

"We understand, don't we?" Marion appealed to her flatmate. "When it's serious you don't want to talk about it, at least in the early stages. It sort of makes you afraid that fate will snatch him away or something, doesn't it? Carol wouldn't talk about Doug, either. I was wondering if he was married or something, she was so secretive about him. Pity it didn't work out. They seemed made for each other. . . . I don't understand what went wrong."

"Carol hasn't mentioned anyone called Doug to me," Nicola said, glad they were off the subject of herself and Jethro, but feeling obliged to stem the flow of confidences about Carol's love life, which she felt was really none of her business.

"How did she seem?"

"All right," Nicola said. "I hadn't seen her for some time, but she seemed fine."

"Well," Marion said doubtfully, "maybe she's getting over it, but she was hard hit at the time. He found someone else, you see, after he and Carol had been going round together for almost a year. Honestly, men are the limit, aren't they? Still, I suppose I shouldn't talk like this to you. You must be badly smitten to have flown over from New Zealand just to be with this guy of yours. It's no use trying to warn you, of course. We all make our own silly mistakes where men are concerned."

Nicola tried another neutral smile, and managed to steer the conversation into other channels.

In the following week she secured two job interviews, which turned out to be not very satisfactory. Neither interviewer had given her a definite answer, but she gathered from one that the position was virtually filled and he was only going through the motions of seeing the remainder of the applicants, and the other was obviously suspicious of her New Zealand background, implying that she was unlikely to treat the job as anything other than a temporary holiday stopgap. It wasn't the first time that had been implied. Usually she hadn't even got as far as a personal interview.

By Thursday she was becoming tired and depressed. She looked up the other address and phone number that Carol had given her. Bettina Yardley wrote for the magazine Carol had worked on. "She's The Bird," Carol had said as she scribbled the address of the magazine's offices.

"What?" Nicola was puzzled.

"The gossip columnist," Carol explained. "Only they don't call it that. It's headed, 'Scene in Sydney, by the Bird,' as in 'a little bird told me,' you know? Awful, isn't it?" she added cheerfully. "Bettina knows absolutely everyone."

Carol had given her only a business number. As Nicola dialed it, she reflected hopefully that if this woman "knew everyone," she might know someone who would give a bookshop assistant from New Zealand a job.

She was put through to Miss Yardley, and a cool, businesslike voice came on the line. "Yes?"

"My name is Nicola Grey," she began. "Carol Lawrence may have written to you about me."

"Oh, yes," the crisp voice said. "How are you getting on? Have you got a place to stay?"

"I'm in a hostel at the moment . . ."

"Good." She sounded relieved. Nicola wondered if she had been afraid of being asked to provide a bed for her. "I'm very tied up this week," Bettina continued, "but there's a sort of semibusiness cocktail party on after work today that I'm supposed to go to. Why don't you come along, and I'll introduce you to a few people."

"That would be nice. Thank you." She needed to meet as many people as possible, if only because one of them might know of a job for her.

"Right. I'll meet you at the G.P.O. in Martin Place, about five-ish. Anyone will direct you."

Nicola had no difficulty finding the Post Office at the hub of the city. Flower-sellers' carts of brilliant blossoms created a splash of colour in the square, contrasting with the sombre reminder of the stone Cenotaph that dominated it, and not far away beyond tall city blocks rose the graceful spire of the Centrepoint Tower. A beautifully groomed and very self-assured young woman wearing a fashionable rust-coloured loose silk tunic and matching scarf over fitted trousers walked briskly up to her. Nicola had already identified her as Bettina before she spoke.

"My car's parked over there," she said. "Illegally, so we'd better move quickly."

It wasn't far to the party, and Bettina drove with a fierce concentration accompanied by occasional muttered expletives that seemed to preclude conversation. She parked expertly, and as they emerged from the car into the street said, "In here," leading the way into a nearby building and up a flight of stairs at the top of which the hum of conversation could be heard. "Did Carol say anything about coming back?" she asked, turning to Nicola.

Nicola shook her head. "I understood she'd resigned her job."

"Yes, but she could get another. With her qualifications . . . she's such a darned good editor. A pity about . . ." Bettina looked at her rather closely. "How well do you know Carol?"

"I know her family very well. We haven't seen much of Carol over the last few years, of course."

"Mm." Bettina looked at her thoughtfully as they reached the top of the stairs. "Well, here we are." She pushed open a glass door, and they entered a large room where several dozen people were standing about talking and drinking.

In five minutes Bettina had introduced her to ten people, and left her with a glass in her hand and a balding man at her side who said he was a travel writer and plied her with questions about New Zealand.

Bettina herself was circulating with the speed of an elegant hurricane, Nicola noticed rather bemusedly, watching from the corner of her eye as the other woman breezed purposefully from group to group. Nicola appreciated that Bettina had taken the time from an obviously busy life to meet her and bring her here, but they had not warmed to each other, and Bettina probably felt she had done her duty to a mere acquaintance of her friend.

She sipped at the last of her drink, and her companion took the glass and said, "Let me get you another."

"Thank you." She watched him thread his way to the bar near the door, and then made a small, surprised sound in her throat. A tall, dark man whose dress jeans and suede jacket emphasised long legs and wide shoulders was standing just inside the glass door, surveying the room. Jethro Vallance.

She felt heat rise to her cheeks, and looked down at the purse she held in her hand. It was silly to be embarrassed at the prospect of facing him just because she had made him a smokescreen for her urge to escape from an awkward situation. But she found his sudden appearance at the party disconcerting. Taking a quick breath, she forced herself to look at him again.

His gaze swept round the room and lighted on her. A faint frown of surprise appeared on his face before he smiled and came across the room.

"Nicola!" he said. "What are you doing in Sydney? I didn't realise that you had plans to come to Australia after the cruise."

"I got itchy feet on that holiday," she told him, trying to sound light. "I'm not ready to settle down yet, and . . . well, I thought I'd like to see something of Australia."

There was a short pause. Then he said, "I see." His glance was keen, and she had the feeling that he had guessed rather accurately at her real reasons. Mercifully, though, he didn't pursue the matter any further. "How long were you thinking of staying?" he asked.

That was something she hadn't really thought about. "I don't know," she said. "Not long," she added ruefully, "if I can't get a job."

"A job? Are you looking for something temporary so that you can take off for the outback or the Gold Coast as soon as you've saved enough?"

Nicola shook her head. "That's what a lot of employers seem to assume, but if I found something decent, I'd stay."

"So this isn't just a working holiday?"

"No."

"What sort of job are you looking for?" he asked.

"I'd like to work with books—it's what I'm used to—but I'll try anything I can get. Beggars can't afford to be choosy. Not that I'm in the beggar class yet, but I don't have unlimited funds, and employment in this city isn't easy to find."

The travel writer came back with her drink, and shortly afterwards, with a faintly resigned look, faded away. Bettina joined them, saying, "You two know each other?"

"We were both on the same cruise ship recently," Jethro said.

Bettina's eyes brightened with curiosity. "I didn't know you'd been on a cruise, Jethro."

"I didn't advertise the fact," Jethro told her somewhat dryly. "I shouldn't think it would interest your readers, anyway."

Bettina smiled. "Where's Justine tonight?"

"She had a previous engagement. Will you excuse me while I get myself a drink?"

As he moved away, Bettina said, "How well do you know him?"

"We were shipboard acquaintances," Nicola said, feeling vaguely uneasy, "that's all. You know how it is."

"Oh, yes." Bettina looked speculative, but didn't ask any more questions. Someone else came over, and soon they were part of a group engaged in general discussion. A little later Nicola noticed a few people leaving, and decided to do the same. She excused herself to Bettina, assuring her she could find her own way home, promising to "keep in touch," and had her hand on the door when Jethro stopped her, his fingers lightly gripping her arm. "Come and see me tomorrow," he said, "at the office. Perhaps I can help. Here's the address."

She took the card he held out to her. "Thank you."

He smiled at her, and suddenly she felt the full force of his masculine charm. Surprised, she wondered if she was getting over Robin at last. She had always realised in a detached way that Jethro was a supremely attractive male, but except for one or two moments of brief awareness on the ship, she had deliberately insulated herself from it. And must continue to do so, she reminded herself. Jethro was engaged to be married to someone called Justine.

A man called Jethro's name, and he said, "Tomorrow," and pushed the door open for her.

Inside the Arcadia offices it was dim and cool, and a thick grey carpet absorbed her footsteps. A pleasant-looking woman at a desk with a crimson leather top asked Nicola for her name and led her into an inner office.

Jethro rose from another crimson-topped desk. He didn't smile, but his voice as he greeted her was welcoming, his eyes intent, darker than she remembered, accentuated by his charcoal business suit. The formal clothes made him somehow less approachable.

He waved her into a deep chair in front of the desk. In the confines of the office he seemed both bigger and more dynamic than he had at the party last night. He sat down and scrutinised her face, his gaze seeming to linger on her mouth. The memory of that kiss they had shared now returned with startling clarity, making her lower her eyes hastily in case he read something in them. With an effort she forced her mind to concentrate on immediate essentials.

"You . . . suggested I come and see you," she began.

"You said you're looking for a job. A permanent one?"

"Yes."

"You're definitely planning to stay in Sydney for some time?"

"Yes," she said again.

He looked down at the large blotter in a leather holder in front of him. "And there's no one back home who could . . . induce you to return?"

He was probing, carefully. She tightened her mouth to stop it trembling betrayingly, looked him straight in the eye, and said very definitely, "No."

For a moment longer he held her gaze. Then he nodded and said, "We're looking for an editorial assistant. It's difficult to find the right sort of person for the position, but I think that you may do."

Hope made her eyes light, but she said cautiously, "I don't have any experience in that line. What makes you think I'd be suitable?"

"It's nothing very arduous or complicated," he assured her. "Mostly it's a matter of common sense, a liking for books and a working knowledge of the English language, plus willingness to work and an ability to use your initiative to some extent. Can you type?"

"Yes. I took typing at school for a year." She wasn't terribly fast, but she could do a letter and knew the right fingers to use on the keys. If he was thinking of giving her a job, she wasn't going to start knocking her own qualifications.

"You could be useful," he said. "I know you've been around books for a few years, and you're able to read and discuss them intelligently. How's your spelling?"

"All right," she said. "Pretty good."

He picked up the phone on his desk and said, "Phoebe, ask Vivienne to come in here for a minute, will you?"

Vivienne was a pretty, well-groomed and friendly-looking woman of around forty, and he introduced her as the fiction editor. "Show Nicola around, tell her what she'd be doing as your assistant, and then bring her back here," he said. "She might take on the job."

It wasn't so complicated. Vivienne's desk in her roomy office was piled with manuscripts from hopeful writers. "They all have to be read," she said.

"Right through?"

Vivienne shook her head. "A few pages are usually enough to tell if they're worth a proper reading. Some are just hopelessly badly written, with no style, appalling grammar, sloppy spelling. They get returned with a rejection letter. That will be part of your job, sending the unwanted ones back to their authors. The better ones are read and assessed carefully. You might get some preliminary reading to do when I'm pressed for time. Don't look so alarmed. It won't be just your decision on which some poor author is rejected. You can give me an opinion before I look at them, that's all. We'll soon find out where we agree and disagree, and you'll learn what to look for. All our submissions are read in house; we don't employ outside readers like some publishers. Jethro insists on that."

Nicola was surprised. "I thought he was only in charge of the financial side," she said. She hadn't imagined he would have any say in editorial decisions.

Vivienne looked surprised, too. "He's in charge of everything," she said. "You know he owns the firm?"

Nicola shook her head.

"Well, he does. He's given the editors a pretty free hand; we do the picking and choosing, but he does like to have the final say. He sees everything before we buy it. This firm was small and respected when he took over after the founder died. He bought it up because the old fellow's relatives weren't interested in carrying it on as a family firm, and now it's one of the fastest growing in the business. We still have a name for quality, and he's guarding that. It was about the only asset he started with, apart from his expertise in accounting, which is what he did before, and his interest in books. But we're gradually acquiring a reputation for backing exciting new writers, too. It's a good place to work."

Nicola felt a stirring of interest. "What else would I have to do?"

"Write a few letters, perhaps do a bit of copy editing, finding typing errors, spelling mistakes, and checking for factual accuracy. Soothe authors who want to know the fate of their manuscript the day after it's delivered. Sharpen blue pencils, maybe." Vivienne shrugged and smiled. "Anything that will save me time, actually. The fiction list is growing rapidly, and we're getting a lot more submissions than when I first took it over. Previously we had a very small interest in fiction, but Jethro decided to build it up, and now that word has gone out we're looking for good novels and new writers, my postbag arrives bulging. Hence my need for an assistant. The title is a euphemism for dogsbody. Still interested?"

"Yes," Nicola said firmly. She would have taken the job if it was heaving bricks because she was desperate for work, but this sounded like an interesting environment with a variety of work to do, and she was sure she was going to enjoy it.

Chapter Three

The job might have been made for her. She quickly learned the office routine, and Jethro, checking on her progress, seemed satisfied with his judgement. No longer the friendly companion of the ship, he was a considerate and courteous employer. Vivienne called him by his first name, but Nicola instinctively addressed him as Mr. Vallance, and although initially he gave her a hard, enigmatic glance, he didn't correct her. She was glad of the slight distance between them, still a little bothered by her new consciousness of him. Once she saw him meet a dark, very sleek and breathtakingly beautiful woman on the steps of the office after work. His fiancée, she supposed, watching enviously.

Knowing she could count on a regular pay packet, she moved in with another New Zealander who had advertised for a flatmate. Amanda was a quiet girl who worked in a solicitor's office, had a boyfriend who called for her regularly but never stayed at the flat, and an almost pathological predilection for privacy. Nicola quite liked her, but she was difficult to know.

Remembering that she had promised Bettina to keep in touch, Nicola phoned her a few days after moving into the flat.

"Nicola!" The voice was much more eager than Nicola had expected. "Where are you? The hostel said you'd left."

"I moved into a flat," Nicola explained, feeling slightly guilty. "And I've got a job." Could Bettina have been genuinely concerned about her?

"Really?" Bettina sounded surprised. "Where?"

"Arcadia Press. It's a publishing firm . . ."

"My dear, I know that! Jethro's firm, of course." She seemed amused now, and Nicola supposed she had been gauche; Bettina, after all, was well up on the Sydney scene. "Well, well. You *are* doing all right!"

"Yes."

"I'll know where to contact you next time," Bettina said. "Arcadia?"

"I'll give you my home number."

Afterward Nicola tried to pinpoint the feeling of unease that the conversation had given her, but there seemed no reason for it. There had been an odd inflection in the woman's voice that made Nicola sense things unsaid.

Some people sounded different on the telephone, their personalities undergoing a subtle change. Probably that was all it was. When she had first spoken to Bettina, she remembered, she had felt that the other woman regarded her as something of nuisance, but she had been quite pleasant when they actually met, in a crisp, impersonal way.

A couple of weeks later, as Vivienne and Nicola were leaving the Arcadia building for lunch, a young woman slammed out of a car drawn up at the curb, sweeping past them and up the steps, so fast and obviously furious that they turned together and stared after her as the doors swung violently closed.

"Good heavens!" Vivienne said. "I wonder what's up with her!"

"It's Jethro's fiancée, isn't it?" Nicola asked.

"Yes. Justine Canham. Oh, well, it's none of our business."

But apparently it was. When they arrived back from lunch Phoebe said, "Oh, Nicola, Mr. Vallance wants to see you in his office. As soon as you get in, he said."

"What have you been up to?" Vivienne asked in amusement.

"Nothing." Nicola smiled in response to the teasing.

"Watch your step," Vivienne admonished humorously as Nicola headed toward the director's office. "Justine looked as though she were spoiling for a fight. He may not be in the best of moods."

He wasn't. That was obvious the moment Nicola closed the door quietly behind her and advanced into the room. He had been standing with his back to her, looking out of the window, and when he swung round she was taken aback. His eyes were dangerously narrowed, and his jaw looked tight, his mouth a hard, uncompromising slash. Nicola stopped in her tracks, her heart beginning to hammer in trepidation. This was neither the easy, pleasant companion of the sea voyage nor the slightly distant employer of more recent weeks. This was a man in an icy but unmistakable temper.

"You wanted me?" she faltered.

"Take a look at this," he said, his words clipped. He picked up a magazine that was opened and folded back, and flung it down on the desk in front of her. "And tell me just what you know about it," he said.

Nicola stared at the page, several photographs among columns of print. She didn't know which paragraph he was bothered about, or what he wanted her to tell him. She looked up. "What?"

His finger stabbed at the page. "That!" he said, and she looked again and felt a sick lurching of her stomach. The photograph he indicated was a small reproduction of the one of her and Jethro on board the cruise ship, the one they had laughed over. Underneath, in bold type, was a caption. She picked up the magazine in shaking fingers and read it.

Up-and-coming publishing tycoon Jethro Vallance and friend living it up aboard the Venus Pacifica *on a recent cruise, soon after the announcement of his engagement to Sydney fashion designer Justine Canham. The lady in the picture is kiwi bird Nicola Grey, now cosily ensconced in a flat in trendy Paddo, and working for Arcadia Press, owned by Guess Who? Wonder what the lovely Justine thinks of it all, folks!*

Nicola read it twice, horror crawling over her skin. She went hot as she forced herself to meet his eyes.

"I . . . I don't know . . ." she croaked, then glanced down at the magazine again and took in the heading at the top. *"Scene in Sydney," by The Bird.*

The colour ebbed from her face and left her feeling cold and clammy. "Bettina!" she whispered.

He said harshly, "Bettina Yardley. A friend of yours, isn't she?"

Dumbly, Nicola shook her head. The movement made her dizzy, and she swayed on her feet.

He made an exasperated sound and came round the desk so quickly that she backed away in alarm. "Don't faint on me!" he said, and grabbed her arm in a paralysing grip to thrust her into a chair. "She said she got this garbage from you! Are you denying it?"

"Yes!" She looked again at the picture, the caption, and said hopelessly, "No. Not exactly. Where did they get the picture?"

"Didn't you provide it?"

"*No!*" This time her denial was vehement, indignant. "I'm sorry, Jethro . . . Mr. Vallance." She studied the caption again with horrified fascination. "It doesn't say . . . anything that isn't true," she said, realising how cleverly the innuendo had been put.

"The implications, however," he said, "are very obvious. Bettina was adamant that those implications came from you."

Nicola closed her eyes in an agony of embarrassment. "I'm sorry," she said again, inadequately.

"Are you admitting it?"

"I . . . in a roundabout way. I didn't expect anything like this . . ."

"So what the hell were you playing at?" he demanded. "Some kind of blackmail? Is that it?"

Nicola's eyes flew open in shock. "Of course not! Surely you don't think . . ."

"I don't know what to think! What on earth did you say to her?"

"I only told her that I had a job here, and a flat. I swear that's all I said . . . to Bettina."

"Do you really expect me to believe that?" he asked witheringly. "Even a muckraker has to have some basis for putting two and two together and making five."

Nicola brushed a strand of hair from her eyes. "Yes, I know . . ."

"So?" He twitched the magazine from her fingers to fling it back on the desk, and leaned against the red leather. "What *do* you know about it?"

She wanted to crawl away into some hole and cover herself up and never come out. She raised her head and made herself look at him. It wasn't easy; he was still furious, but he waited patiently for her answer.

"I think," she said, "it was something I said back home. To my family. A friend of ours was there at the time. She used to work for the magazine, and she wrote to Bettina about me. She gave me Bettina's name as a contact here, you see, because I didn't know anyone in Sydney."

"And that's all?" he raised his brows skeptically. "Something you said? I'd like to know what it was."

Avoiding his eyes, she said, "Does it matter? Can't we just ask the magazine to set the record straight? If we both deny it . . ."

"Oh, sure. We'll tell them we're just good friends, shall we? Act your age, woman!" Without pausing for breath, he returned to the attack. "You haven't told me what it was you said that led people to this interesting conclusion about your relationship with me."

Nicola looked down at her hands. "I . . . let them think," she said, "that I was coming to Sydney to be with you. That we were . . . romantically involved."

His breath drew in audibly. Hard hands seized her upper arms, dragging her out of the chair to stand in front of him. *"Say that again!"* he ordered, his voice dangerously quiet.

"I'm sorry!" she said desperately. "I didn't think you'd ever know. It wasn't meant to go outside my family. I didn't realise that Bettina would . . . Carol must have told her something in her letter. I swear I didn't say anything to her directly. It's all hearsay."

He made a sharp exclamation under his breath and let her go, leaving her rubbing at her arms as he strode over to the window again and stood for a moment with his back to her. Then he turned and said, "Why? What on earth did you do it for?"

"Pride, really. It's not easy to explain, but it seemed like a good idea at the time. Just before I went on that holiday, I'd been jilted by the man I thought I was going to marry. That was the reason for the cruise. My family were all sympathy for me, and they just overwhelmed me with kindness. I thought being away from them for a bit would help. When I got back, everything seemed just the same. I felt that I couldn't take any more pity . . . or any more reminders. Someone saw that photograph and asked who you were, and of course they . . . teased. I let them jump to conclusions. I wanted to get away again, and the answer seemed to be to . . . to allow everyone to assume I was coming here to be with the man in the photograph. I would have written home in a few weeks telling them it hadn't worked out, but meantime I wanted to stay in Sydney. There seemed no reason why you should ever know."

"And what I didn't know couldn't hurt me?" he enquired sarcastically.

"It was wrong of me. I realise you and Miss Canham must be furious; I don't blame you."

"That's an understatement," he said grimly.

"I'll see the editor of the magazine," she offered. "They'll have to print a retraction if I make some sort of statement of what really happened."

For a moment the anger in his face altered to a kind of hard curiosity. "Would you be willing for them to print a statement like that?"

She winced, thinking of the humiliation she would suffer, the pity and scorn such a public confession would incite. "Yes," she said steadily. "It was my fault, and I have to do what I can to rectify the damage."

"That might be difficult. For one thing, I don't see them doing it. As you pointed out, they've been careful to print nothing but actual facts."

"I'll try," she promised.

"Don't bother," he advised her tersely. "I'm not particularly concerned anyway about the opinion of a pulp journalist and her readers." He paused. "What you can do," he said slowly, "is come with me and explain to my fiancée."

"But didn't you do that?" she asked involuntarily.

He gave her a cold look. "Naturally."

His mouth closed firmly, and she said, shocked, "You mean she didn't believe you?"

He took something from his pocket and placed it carefully on the desk. "I should have said my *ex*-fiancée."

"Oh, no!" Nicola stared at the gold band with the square-cut ruby flanked by diamonds. "I'm terribly s—"

"Don't say you're sorry again," he interrupted. "We'll take that as read, shall we?"

Nicola swallowed.

He picked up the phone, dialed, and asked for Miss Canham. "Yes, it is Mr. Vallance," he said a moment later. Then, "That's all right. Thank you."

He put down the phone and said, "Miss Canham is not receiving calls from me at the moment. We'll make it after work. It might be better at her home, anyway. Wait for me at five, will you?"

"Yes, of course." She could, for all he knew, have been doing something tonight, but in any case she would have cancelled it. She was appalled at what her supposedly innocent deception had caused, and would do anything to put it right and square her conscience.

Sitting in the dark blue Jaguar as Jethro negotiated the rush-hour traffic, she stared out the window, trying to think of what she could say to Justine Canham, gathering her courage. A dull orange glow was reflected onto the street by the plate-glass windows of the tall office blocks as the sun threw its light on them. The day was still warm, and the heat, combined with the roar of the traffic as workers streamed homeward in their thousands by car or underground rail, was giving her a headache.

Jethro steered the big car expertly through narrow streets with their mixture of old and new buildings, and onto thoroughfares where the squat, baroque colonial structures had been bulldozed to make way for high-rises.

Speaking her thoughts aloud, Nicola said, "I *didn't* give them that photograph. Where could they have got it from?"

Jethro's glance was impatient. "Probably from the shipping company. It wouldn't be difficult."

She supposed not. Bettina was no doubt accustomed to following up small clues. The passenger list would show Jethro's name—and hers. And the ship's photographer would have been willing enough to sell the print. That was his job. What a mess, she thought wearily, massaging her temples with her fingers.

Jethro looked at her bowed head and said abruptly, "Are you all right?"

"Yes." She dropped her hand, gazing straight ahead. She wasn't angling for pity. She had got herself into this. Unfortunately she had got him into it too, and that was inexcusable. It was bad luck that Jethro was more newsworthy than she had realised, that Carol's friend Bettina was a gossip columnist and wouldn't let slip a chance to pick up on a trivial bit of information. But the first mistake had been her own. She had lied by implication, and now she was paying for it. This interview would be embarrassing and unpleasant, but she just had to grit her teeth and get it over with.

It was worse than she had imagined. When Justine opened the door and saw Jethro, she tried to close it again, but he pushed it wide against her resistance and walked in, his hand on Nicola's arm dragging her with him before he shut the door decisively behind them.

Justine was wearing a wine-coloured lounging gown that accentuated her striking colouring. She looked beautiful and furious, her dark eyes flashing stormily.

"Justine," Jethro said, "this is Nicola Grey."

As Justine's eyes lighted disbelievingly on Nicola, sheer hatred distorted the perfect features. She transferred her malevolent gaze to Jethro and spat, *"How dare you!* How *dare* you bring your cheap little mistress here!"

Nicola's chin went up, and Jethro said evenly, "Nicola is not my mistress. Sit down."

"*Don't* you tell me to sit down in my own home!" Her voice was shrill with rage.

Jethro, obviously reining in his own temper, said, "Nicola has something to say to you. Please sit down."

"No!" She made swiftly for the phone that sat on a low table next to the long, luxurious sofa set against one wall. "I'll give you ten seconds to get out of here, then I'm calling the police."

Jethro gave a crack of angry laughter. "Don't be so melodramatic!" he snapped, and strode across the room, catching her wrist and taking the receiver from her to replace it on the cradle. She made a futile swipe at him with her other hand which he dodged, pushing her down forcibly on the sofa.

"You brute!" Justine said hoarsely. "When I do get hold of the police there'll be an assault charge to add to one of forcible entry!"

"Shut up," Jethro said, "and listen. Nicola, come here."

Nicola walked across the room as though treading on broken glass. She stood before the other woman and forced herself to meet that dark, vindictive gaze.

"I came to apologise, Miss Canham," she said quietly.

"For sleeping with my fiancé behind my back? Well, that's handsome of you!"

"Be quiet!" Jethro ordered. "Give the girl a chance to explain."

"Explain? What's to explain? You're such a stud you couldn't do without a woman for a few weeks, and this little slut was obviously available. I do think you might have done better for yourself, though, darling. . . ." Her eyes disparagingly assessed Nicola. "You obviously weren't spoiled for choice. . . ."

"That's enough!" The whipcrack of his voice would have silenced anyone. Justine's brightly glossed mouth tightened into a hard, ugly line, and she turned her head away disdainfully as though she had no intention of listening to anything either of them might say, but she didn't speak.

"Go on, Nicola," Jethro said.

Nicola wished she were anywhere else. "That report was untrue," she said stoically. "Someone jumped to conclusions, and I'm afraid that it's my fault."

Justine continued to ignore her while she went determinedly on, explaining about the photograph, her return home, and all the rest of the chain of circumstances that had led to the paragraph in the gossip column.

At last she came to a stop, and Justine swept one scornful look at her and said, "Have you finished?"

"Yes," Nicola said huskily. "Except to offer my sincerest apology. I had no idea that anything like this could happen."

Justine looked at her as one might look at a creature that had crawled out of a ditch. "Is that all you can say?"

Nicola said, "I know it's inadequate. I've told Jethro

—Mr. Vallance—that I'm willing to ask the magazine to print a statement from me. If there's anything else I can do . . . believe me, I really am dreadfully sorry."

"It's a bit late for that!" Justine got to her feet in a quick, agitated movement. "You've made a public fool of me, you stupid, mealy-mouthed little liar . . ."

"Justine!"

But she took no notice of Jethro this time. Her fury in full spate, she called Nicola worse than that, appalling things that made Nicola cringe, not so much in fear as in embarrassment for the other woman's loss of control, until Jethro stepped in between them, took Justine by the shoulders and shook her, saying, *"For God's sake, Justine!"*

She looked up at him, breathing hard, her face flushed. "She deserves it! We could sue her for this! All my friends read that magazine . . . How do you think I felt when Claudia brought it to me, the cat! She's always been jealous of me, ever since we were at school. How she enjoyed it, pretending to sympathise! Have you any idea how it feels to be humiliated like that?"

Jethro didn't answer. He released his grip, and Justine glanced at Nicola, then looked back at him, making an obvious effort to curb her temper. "Well," she said, "I have to believe her, I suppose. I can't imagine any woman admitting to such a story if it wasn't true, no matter how much you were willing to pay her, or how infatuated she was with you."

Jethro said in a strange voice, "Is that all you have to say?"

For a moment Justine looked nonplussed. Then she gave an artificial little laugh and said, "You want an apology? All right, darling, I'm sorry I doubted you, though you must admit that I had very good reason. *Miss* Grey can count herself lucky if I don't sue her for malicious slander, the lying little tramp. And now, I'll accept my ring back from you." She looked at him expectantly, a little smile curving her beautiful mouth.

Jethro stayed where he was, surveying her with an expressionless face. "I don't think so," he said slowly. Justine's eyes widened, and Nicola, trying to stay in the background, suppressed a gasp of shock.

Justine laughed again, on a rather higher note than before. "Don't be silly, darling! I'm not the one who should be punished. I suppose you're offended because I didn't believe you right away, but really, Jethro, what else could I think? You must be reasonable!"

"You weren't being very reasonable when you threw the ring in my face earlier."

"Do you blame me?" she said with exasperation. "I was angry . . . and . . ."—her eyes swept down, and tears trembled on her lashes—". . . and hurt."

Nicola said softly, "She's right, you can't blame her . . ."

Justine turned on her, her eyes flashing again through gleaming tears. "You keep out of this!" she said shrilly. "You've done enough damage already, you bitch!"

Jethro's mouth tightened. He fished in his pocket and brought out his keys. "Here," he said to Nicola. "Wait for me in the car."

Nicola thankfully left the apartment, glad to get outside into the fresh air. She found the right key after several tries and sat in the car, so tense that her neck and shoulders ached.

Jethro joined her about fifteen minutes later. She said, "If you want to stay with Miss Canham, I can get a bus or something."

He started the car without answering, and she didn't argue. The district was strange to her, and she had no idea how to go about getting public transport to where she lived.

"Paddington, isn't it?"

"Not really," she said. "It's on the border between Paddington and Glebe." She had already learned that Paddington, or Paddo, was one of the more desirable suburbs. Though a working-class district in the nineteenth century, its terraced houses and gracious old villas in steep, tree-lined streets had been taken over by professional people with money to spend on restoring them and furnishing them in a style that would have dazzled the original owners. Glebe, nestled between the harbour and the sprawling campus of the university, was less expensive, with a large proportion of students in its population, but its architecture was equally interesting, the skyline broken by turreted roofs, the houses featuring delicately wrought iron latticework, the shops a cosmopolitan mixture often operated by "New Australians" from Greece, Italy, and many other European and Asian countries.

Jethro drove in silence for some time, then said abruptly, "You haven't eaten, have you?"

Startled, she said, "No." Neither had he, of course, but she didn't see the relevance of the question.

"We'll find a restaurant and have a meal."

She looked at him doubtfully, considerably surprised. "Surely that isn't a very good idea?"

He looked at her with hard eyes, gave a brief mirthless laugh, and said, "It's the best idea I've had all day."

He found a small Spanish place that had an atmosphere of Mediterranean warmth and where the service was efficient and fast. The proprietor himself appeared as they were finishing their meal, and enquired anxiously, with a thick Spanish accent, whether everything was satisfactory.

"Fine, thanks," Jethro answered. "The paella was excellent."

Nicola, who had settled for a Spanish omelette and a salad with olives and cheese, echoed his satisfaction.

"Coffee?" the proprietor offered, and Jethro said, "Perhaps some more wine, first."

They had already finished a small carafe between them as they ate, and Nicola cast a searching glance at Jethro as a second one was placed on the table.

Jethro filled their glasses and lifted his own, surveying her rather sardonically. "Don't look so worried," he said. "I'm not going to drown my sorrows in drink."

Nicola lowered her eyes, picking up her glass. His manner throughout the meal had been offhand and rather grim. He didn't seem like a man who had just been through a reconciliation scene with his fiancée. She wondered what had happened in the flat after she left. She drank some of the wine and asked, "Is everything all right now?"

"What?" He had been staring without expression at a picture of a matador at the moment of the kill, the red cape floating with deceptive grace above the animal's bent head as the sword penetrated its massive neck.

"Miss Canham," she said. "Did you give back her ring?"

"No." He put down his half-empty glass and filled it to the brim, his movements very deliberate.

"Don't you think that you're being rather harsh? That photograph looks so . . ."

He shrugged. "I'd have thought," he said, "that as my fiancée she would have accepted my word against that of a gutter journalist. Wouldn't you?"

She didn't think that if she loved someone she would have refused to believe his denial, but she wasn't Justine. "I don't know," she said. "It must have been quite a shock for her."

"You're more generous than she was to you."

Nicola looked down at her glass. "I'm the one at fault. She had reason to be upset."

He gave a faint grin, suddenly. "She did give an impressive rendition of a woman scorned, didn't she?"

Nicola just stopped herself from smiling back. It didn't seem right for her to be laughing with him at Justine, who was, after all, a woman wronged, if not exactly scorned.

She said, "I'm sure she regrets having doubted your word. When you give her ring back you'll find everything is all right."

He poured some more wine and drank it. "I'm not giving it back. The engagement is over. She was the one who broke it, after all."

"But she's changed her mind!"

"So have I. I won't go into a marriage without trust. Justine didn't trust me, didn't believe in me."

"She was upset. She's obviously got a quick temper."

"And a nasty one. I'm sorry I let you in for that tongue-lashing."

She shook her head and said in a low voice, "I expect she was right. I deserved it."

"No." He paused. In a quite different tone he said, "In all this contretemps, no one has taken *your* feelings into consideration, have they?"

She looked up in surprise, and he said, "Apart from the embarrassment of being found out in a deception, I mean. You have a broken engagement behind you, too. You're still feeling pretty raw, aren't you?"

She nodded, saying huskily, "I'll get over it."

"Yes," he said. "We both will."

He asked for coffee and drank it in moody silence. Nicola didn't finish hers.

As he drew the car up outside her flat, Nicola tried again. "You might feel differently in the morning.

You're bitter at the moment, but it wasn't such a crime, you know. I'm sure that Justine—Miss Canham—"

"No chance," he said flatly. "Leave it, will you?"

"I can't. Surely if you love her . . ."

"It's none of your business, Nicola."

"Yes it is. I feel responsible."

"Well, that's your bad luck," he said almost gently. "Some things can't be undone."

"But . . ."

"I said, leave it!" He leaned over suddenly and dropped a brief, hard kiss on her mouth, shocking her into silence. "Now stop worrying about it and get inside," he said. "There's nothing more you can do, and if you want to know, Justine and I have both probably had a narrow escape."

"You can't have ever loved her!" she exclaimed.

He shrugged again and said indifferently, "Perhaps not. What's your definition of love?"

"Well, it includes forgiveness!"

"Have you forgiven your lover for deserting you?"

She was silent. She had tried not to think about Robin, but when she did, mingled with the pain was a tight, hard knot of jealous, resentful anger. No, she hadn't forgiven him for his faithlessness. She couldn't.

He laughed shortly and leaned over to open the car door for her. "I'll see you in the morning," he said.

Nicola fumbled as she put her key in the door of the flat. He waited until she was inside before driving off.

She touched her mouth, still tingling from the effects of that rather rough, exasperated but strangely comforting kiss. Her headache was thunderous now, and although it was surprisingly not very late, she took a couple of aspirins, had a bath and went to bed. The events of the day replayed themselves in disjointed fashion behind her closed lids. Jethro flinging the magazine in front her; her horrified comprehension of

what had happened; Justine screaming insults; Jethro
saying, "What's your definition of love?" Images of
what she had not seen intruded. Justine pleading with
him, her dark eyes tearful, asking to be forgiven, and
Jethro, with a tight, cruel look, saying, "You didn't
trust me, did you? It's over."

And then herself with Jethro in the car, and him
suddenly bending toward her and kissing her. It was the
last image before she finally slept.

Chapter Four

"You'll be at the launching of Jess Seymour's *Prisoners in Petticoats* next week, won't you?" Vivienne asked as she handed Nicola a manuscript to be returned to its hopeful owner.

"Yes, I'm looking forward to meeting her," Nicola answered. She had read a couple of chapters and skimmed the remainder of the proofs when they were returned by the printer, and had found the book fascinating, a historical novel of the women of one family from the time of the early settlers to the present day.

Nicola arrived early at the reception because Vivienne had warned her that as a matter of courtesy Jethro expected his staff to be punctual, and she was introduced to the author and her husband before the majority of the invited guests made their appearances. Jess was a tall brunette with a warm, low voice that underlined the ironic humour that ran through her conversation like a sparkling thread. In contrast to her, Gareth Seymour was a quiet, slender man who appeared at first almost self-effacing, but Nicola caught him looking at his wife with an expression compounded of pride and amused understanding, and when, apparently sensing Nicola's eyes on him, he turned to meet them, she was surprised at the acuity in his light blue gaze. He moved to her side as his wife was accosted by a new arrival, and with a faint smile and a glance at her name label he said, "How long have you been working at Arcadia?"

"Less than two months. I've read a little of your wife's book. It's very good."

"I hope you'll tell her that. I never imagined that Jess's ego was so fragile until I saw how nervous she is about whether her book is any good or not."

"It is!" Nicola said. "I'm sure of it. We wouldn't be publishing it if it wasn't."

He smiled at her with real friendliness. "That's company loyalty, I suppose. Still, it's what I've been telling Jess."

Jethro came up with two glasses of white wine in his hands and passed one to Nicola, asking, "Want one?"

She took it, a little disconcerted. It was nice of him to notice that she didn't have a drink, but ever since she had accompanied him to Justine's flat, she had felt constrained in his presence. Sometimes in the office she found him looking at her with an oddly frowning expression, and she thought that although he was too fair-minded to ask her to leave, and perhaps also too obstinate to let emotion influence his actions in business, she reminded him of unpleasantness and even heartache that he would prefer to forget. She had tried to keep out of his way as much as possible.

She sipped the drink, her easy manner deserting her. The men talked for a while, and she took the first opportunity that she could to murmur an excuse and go to join Vivienne, who was standing with a tall, startlingly handsome older man. He had arrived looking rather forbidding, but his expression had melted into a perfectly dazzling smile as soon as he saw Vivienne. Nicola, unable to resist a curious glance at Vivienne's face, had seen her colour faintly as she gave the man a much more restrained smile in return. Now she was laughing, and he was regarding her with eyes that held an unmistakable message of male admiration. Vivienne was looking particularly attractive in a pink chiffon dress that combined sophistication with femininity, and her companion's every glance confirmed it.

Vivienne introduced him as Pietro Benotti, and for a few seconds as he took Nicola's hand in his and smiled into her eyes, she experienced the full battery of his Italian charm. It seemed that he had been the one to introduce Jess to Vivienne when she had barely started on her book, and he was teasingly claiming a large share of responsibility for its being published.

"All right, so you introduced Jess to me," Vivienne said, "and we're both grateful, I'm sure. It's been a fruitful partnership."

"Won't you grant me a partnership in the enterprise too? Perhaps a sleeping one?" Pietro inquired wickedly.

Vivienne almost choked on her drink, and Nicola bit her lip, trying to keep a straight face. But Pietro's expression, except for an amused gleam at the back of his eyes, was one of bland enquiry. "Well?" he said gently.

Vivienne shook her head. "You don't qualify."

Pietro's brows rose. His voice silkily seductive, he said, "Tell me what I have to do."

But Vivienne said evasively, "I've got to talk to someone over there . . . excuse me."

He smiled after her as she moved away, but his eyes had narrowed a little. When the smile disappeared he looked quite formidable, and he wasn't even trying to disguise his intentions. Nicola felt that any woman would find him hard to resist, also that he wouldn't be likely to easily take no for an answer, and she wondered what Vivienne thought about his blatant interest in her.

He turned, and as though reading Nicola's thoughts, said, "She's a delightful lady. You work with her?"

"Yes. For the last few weeks."

He bent toward her, looking as though the information was fascinating in the extreme, and plied her with questions until she only just stopped herself from telling him her reasons for departing from New Zealand. He certainly had a way with him, she thought, bemused. Even with her, he managed to drop a few deft compliments in the course of the conversation. But she had the impression that Vivienne had aroused considerably more than the passing admiration for any woman that seemed to come naturally to him.

After speeches had been made, and Jess had signed copies of her book for those who bought them on the spot, Nicola was looking for an opportunity to unobtrusively leave, when a hand touched her elbow. Jethro, said, "How are you getting home?"

"By bus," she replied, surprised.

"Wait for me," he said. "I'll take you."

Before she could reply, he had gone away through the crowd to speak to someone else. She really had no choice but to wait as he had instructed her.

He, of course, had to stay until the end, and when Jess and Gareth had left he returned to Nicola and said, "Ready?"

He put his hand on her waist and guided her to the lift and down to the hotel car park.

"Enjoy yourself?" he asked her as he swung the car into the road.

"Yes, thank you. I liked Jess, and there were some interesting people there."

"I saw you talking to that Italian bloke." He threw her a glance. "You seemed to be getting on like a house on fire."

"He's very charming."

He made a sound that was suspiciously like a grunt, and stopped for a red light, his fingers drumming on the wheel until the signal changed to green.

"You didn't need to bring me home," she said.

"I wanted to."

"That's kind of you, but . . ."

"I said, I *wanted* to. That isn't being kind."

Nicola looked at him somewhat cautiously. "Why?"

For a few moments he didn't answer, his foot on the accelerator making the car pick up speed. Then he said, "I have the impression that you've been avoiding me lately."

Surprised and wary, she said, "Of course I haven't. I couldn't, anyway. We work in the same office."

"Perhaps that's why it's been so noticeable. You *have* been avoiding me, haven't you?"

The blunt accusation threw her. "Not . . . exactly," she muttered. "Anyway, it can't be important . . . to you."

Again it was a few moments before he replied. "It's a small office. We've always maintained a friendly atmosphere. And"—he suddenly sounded irritable, "I don't like being treated like a pariah."

"I haven't . . ."

"Yes, you have. Vivienne's commented on it. She thought you were shy—with men. You weren't at all shy tonight . . . nor on the cruise."

"That was different. You're my employer now."

"I'm Vivienne's employer too. That doesn't stop us from enjoying a friendly relationship."

"I don't think there's any law that says employer and employee relationships have to be friendly, is there?"

She had spoken more sharply than she had intended, and he looked at her quickly before returning his attention to the road.

Defensively, she said, "If you think I've been . . . discourteous . . . I'm sorry. It wasn't intentional."

"You know perfectly well you're the soul of courtesy. But that's all you give . . . cold courtesy. There's no warmth in it."

"What do you *want?*"

Again he glanced briefly at her. Then, his eyes fixed on the road ahead, he said slowly, "On the ship, we were friends. That's gone. And I want it back."

A faint shock rippled through her. "The circumstances were different."

"You're still the same person," he insisted. "I know you've had a 'disappointment in love,' but that obviously hasn't changed your attitude to all men. You were able to relate to me without any strain on that holiday, and you were doing fine with Gareth Seymour and that Italian, so why am I singled out now for special treatment?"

"I don't know what you mean."

"Yes, you do," he said shortly. "You're not stupid. And I'm not paranoid."

Helplessly, she shrugged. Her voice low, she said reluctantly, "For one thing, you're my employer, and I don't think I was the only one who was being aloof. And, if you must know, I feel . . . uncomfortable with you, after . . . that scene with you and your fiancée."

"Ex-fiancée," he corrected instantly. "Is that all?"

"Yes."

He was silent for a long time, until he stopped the car outside her flat. Then, as she reached for the door handle, he caught her wrist and said, "Don't run away."

"I wasn't."

She tried to ease her wrist out of his hold, but his grip tightened by a fraction, and he said, "Let's talk this out. It wasn't pleasant for you, that evening. I admired your self-control, and I'm sorry that I let you in for Justine's histrionics. Apparently she has a taste for emotion that I never suspected before, and she was determined to wring every scrap of drama out of the whole thing. Obviously you didn't enjoy the experience. But does it matter that much?"

She wished he would let go. His fingers encircling her wrist were warm and strong, and his thumb was now absently stroking the back of her hand. She was altogether too aware of him. She shook her head slightly, not so much in reply to his question as in an effort to clear confusion from her thoughts.

"Then can't we be friends again?" he asked her quietly, and a finger came under her chin, turning her towards him.

In the dim light from the streetlamps he looked grave and questioning and very close. Warning bells were ringing in her mind. But she didn't move, mesmerised by his eyes, his voice, the subtle spell of attraction that emanated from him. When he bent his head she closed her eyes and waited for the kiss that was inevitable.

When it came, it was light and warm and extremely gentle, but it made her pulses throb, and she curled her fingers in her lap to stop herself from responding to it.

He drew away a little, and his hands cupped her head, his fingers in her hair. She saw the purpose in his face as he made to kiss her again, and she said, "No."

He sat very still, looking down at her. "Why not?"

Nicola moistened her lips with her tongue and said huskily, "I don't want you to."

His hands tightened fractionally, his thumbs moving on her cheeks, and for a moment she thought he was going to ignore her protest. Then his shoulders lifted and he released her. Resting a forearm on the curve of the steering wheel, he sat looking at her speculatively. "It isn't that you don't like it, is it?" he asked. "What's the matter?"

"I don't go in for casual kisses," she said. "You ought to know that. Thank you for bringing me home, Mr. Vallance."

This time she managed to get the door open and slip out quickly. Even so, he was out of the car and by her side as she reached the steps. "Just one thing," he said, as she put the key in the lock and turned it. "You can stop calling me Mr. Vallance."

As she made to open the door, he put his hand on it and prevented her from swinging it wide, so that she was trapped by his arm. She kept her eyes on the sleeve of his jacket. "Is that an order?"

"If you like." He sounded rather fed up, his voice clipped.

"All right," she said. "May I go in now?"

He removed his arm, and she stepped into the hallway and closed the door. After a few seconds she heard the engine of his car start again and he drove off. Only then did she move away from the door and go up to her room.

He couldn't, she thought, order her to be friendly. She meticulously addressed him by his first name from then on, but the feelings that he had so effortlessly aroused in her were a danger sign. She wasn't ready for an involvement on the rebound, and especially not with a man who was in the same situation as herself. More especially, she told herself firmly, not with Jethro, who was positively callous with women. Even on the ship there had been evidence of it. He could have shown Rita a bit of sympathy and spent some time with her while making it clear that he was not free, but he had chosen instead to use Nicola as a smoke screen. He had charm when he wanted to exert it, and she had not realised then the essentially selfish nature of his actions. But having seen the ruthless way he dealt with Justine and her suspicions, she decided that allowing herself to succumb to his casual attraction would be asking for trouble.

When he spoke to her at work she answered succinctly and politely, but she seldom looked at him directly and always turned back to her work as soon as she had dealt with his query or command. She was aware that he watched her whenever they were in the same room; she could feel it as an electric tingling on her skin, and if she glanced fleetingly at him, it was to see a baffled and irritated expression in his eyes.

Vivienne said to her once, "You haven't quarrelled with Jethro, have you, Nicola?"

"No."

"Don't you like him?"

"He's my employer," Nicola said. "It doesn't matter if I like him or not, does it?"

"I take it that means no," Vivienne said. "I wonder why? I thought that you'd been quite friendly before you came to work here."

"We . . . knew each other slightly," Nicola said. "That's all."

Vivienne cast her a curious look but said no more. Nicola wondered if she had read Bettina's column, but if she had, she obviously wasn't going to mention it.

Jethro stopped by her desk one day when Vivienne was out of the office. "I have an invitation for you," he said.

"For me?" She looked up, straight into his eyes for once.

"To a party," he said, "at Jess and Gareth Seymour's."

"But they hardly know me!"

"They'll remember you," he said. "You're coming as my partner. I'll pick you up on Thursday night at eight."

He turned to leave, and astonishment almost held her silent, but as he reached the door she said, "Jethro?"

He looked round, his hand on the door handle, his brows raised interrogatively, obviously impatient.

"Do you mean . . . this is a social invitation?"

"Jess is one of our authors," he said. "That makes it business."

He was gone before she could protest any more.

He picked her up promptly when he had said, and she was ready on time, not wanting to keep him waiting.

As he opened the passenger door of the car his gaze swept comprehensively over her and approved the full-skirted deep gold dress with its narrow bronze belt, and the bronze high-heeled pumps.

"You look good," he said as he slid into his seat, giving her another glance.

There hadn't been many social occasions for her since coming to Sydney; she had avoided dating and going out in the evenings. The opportunity to dress up a little, and the prospect of meeting interesting people and enjoying their company, were suddenly appealing. She must be getting over Robin, beginning to look outward instead of licking her wounds in private.

All the same, she had reservations about this evening. She wasn't sure why Jethro had elected to make her his partner.

He didn't talk much as he drove, and when he drew up outside a modern apartment block overlooking the harbour, he got out immediately and came round to help her out, then with his hand on her waist guided her up the steps into the building.

The apartment was on the fourth floor, and the lounge, furnished in grey and rich brown with touches of emerald and gold, opened onto a balcony overlooking the water. Only a few people were there before them. Jess introduced them, and Gareth smiled at Nicola as he handed her a drink, saying, "Nice to see you again, Nicola."

She said, "I'm surprised you remember my name. You must have met a lot of people at the launching."

"Of course I remember it."

Jess said, "He doesn't forget beautiful girls, Nicola," and her husband turned and gave her one of his coolly amused looks. "Naturally," he agreed, and she saw a smiling glance pass between them.

The doorbell rang, and Jess admitted Vivienne and Pietro Benotti.

"I told him I could find my own way," Vivienne was saying as Jess brought them into the living room, "but he would insist on collecting me."

"She was determined to be difficult," Pietro commented. "Career women are so afraid to relinquish one iota of their independence. As if it would undermine their liberation."

Nicola noted the slight flush on Vivienne's cheeks, and tension in Pietro's gleaming smile. Sensing an undercurrent, she wondered if they had quarrelled. Then she saw Pietro look at Vivienne again, and there was something softer in his dark eyes, perhaps a hint of apology.

A young couple arrived with a toddler who was put in a bedroom to sleep. Its mother was Pietro's stepdaughter Claire, her husband a strikingly handsome, fair man called Scott Carver. They and the Seymours were evidently good friends. The room was filling now, and Jethro eventually gave up the chair he had been sitting on to one of the women, coming to perch on the broad arm of Nicola's. She was listening to Claire, the mother of the baby, talk about her experience of teaching on a tiny Pacific island before she married, but as Jethro placed his arm along the back of her chair, his jacket sleeve brushing her neck, Nicola lost the thread of the conversation. It was several minutes before she was able to relax and ignore the fact that he was sitting so close to her.

Claire began to question her about New Zealand, her eyes alight with interest. "You must come to dinner one night," she suggested.

"Thank you, I'd like that." Nicola had warmed to the other woman, and was pleased that Claire seemed to like her.

"You too, Jethro," Claire said, smiling up at him.

"Thanks," he said, his hand straying to Nicola's shoulder. "I'll look forward to it."

The baby woke, and Claire went off to soothe him, coming back into the room later with the child in her arms. Several women gathered round to admire and talk to him, and after a few moments Jethro said in Nicola's ear, "Don't you want to go and coo at the infant, too?"

She shook her head. "Not specially."

Curiously he asked, "Don't you like babies?"

Nicola looked up at him. "Do you?"

He looked surprised, and then laughed. "I like kids . . . the kind that talk intelligibly."

"I'm much the same," she confessed. "Little babies don't have a lot of conversation."

"True," he conceded. "You might feel different about your own offspring, though."

"So might you," she retorted, making him laugh again, and for a few minutes they almost regained the casual rapport they had shared on the ship.

The baby toddled about exploring for a while, occasionally steadied by willing hands and watched by his parents. As Claire laughingly scooped him away from a glass someone had left on a low table, Jess took a chair close to Nicola and Jethro, saying, "Isn't it marvelous? Claire was terribly ill before she had him—we were all worried sick—but you'd never know it to look at them both now."

"They make a lovely picture," Jethro agreed blandly.

Jess looked at him sharply, then laughed. "Okay, I'll stop clucking," she promised. "I'll bet Nicola doesn't share your cynical outlook, though."

"Who's cynical?" Jethro protested mildly. "I'm consumed with envy, actually."

Jess looked decidedly skeptical, her green eyes studying him with considerable irony, then narrowing a little. Nicola realised she was weighing the possibility that he was serious. Perhaps, Nicola thought, he had looked forward to having children with Justine. It was hard to imagine Justine as a mother, but then she hadn't been at her sweetest when Nicola had met her.

Later, although there wasn't a great deal of room, people began dancing. Jethro pulled her to her feet and onto the floor among the swaying couples. Nicola held herself rigid, and he looked down at her in surprise. "What's the trouble?" he asked. "You're a good dancer, but you've gone as stiff as a board."

"I'm out of practice," she said, trying to relax.

Someone turned down the lights, and a few people

laughed. Jethro placed both hands on her waist, pulling her closer, but she strained away from him.

He gave an impatient sigh, and she said, "I'm sorry. I don't feel like dancing. It's a bit stuffy."

"Okay, let's go outside."

She hadn't meant that, but they were not far from the curtained glass door that opened onto the balcony, and in a moment she found herself standing out there with him, the distant lights creating shimmering ribbons on the harbour, and a faint hum of traffic reverberating in the background.

She went to the concrete parapet and put her hands on it, looking out at the satin blackness of the water and the sparkle of the lights. She was aware of Jethro watching her, and after a while he came and stood just behind her and said, "I wish you'd tell me what's going on."

"There isn't anything going on."

His hand cupped her shoulder. She felt that he was just stopping himself from gripping hard. His voice deliberately even, he said, "We had a good time, you and I, on the cruise, didn't we?"

"Yes," she acknowledged.

"Then surely we can do so again? Isn't that just what we both need? It's the accepted cure for a broken romance."

"Off with the old and on with the new?" she asked dryly. "No, thank you. I'm not like that."

"How do you know?" His hand moved on her shoulder caressingly. "If you shut yourself off from every new experience, keep nursing your hurt, it'll never heal."

"I'm doing all right."

"You're doing your best to turn yourself into some sort of Sleeping Beauty," he said, his voice roughening.

Shaking off his hand, she turned to face him.

"What's it to you? Are you sore because I turned down that pass you made the other night?"

His mouth hardened, and a flash of anger lit his eyes. Then, unexpectedly, he said, "Yes, I suppose I am. I'm sore at being treated like some casual Lothario who's trying to make it with you. I'm sore that you don't trust me."

"Of course I trust you!"

"You do?" he asked with sarcasm. "Is that why you iced up when I kissed you . . . why you can't dance with me anymore . . . why you're afraid to let me put my arms around you?"

"You're talking nonsense."

He said, "What do I have to do to get *through* to you?"

"Why should you want to?" she cried, bewildered.

For a moment he looked almost taken aback. Then someone pushed aside the curtains and stepped onto the balcony, saying gaily, "Oh, sorry, are we interrupting?"

Jethro stepped back, and Nicola brushed hastily past him and said, "No, of course not," as she hastened back into the room. She heard Jethro mutter as he followed her, "Not at all," and then his hand was on her arm and he was saying, "Let's go, shall we?"

She knew he wouldn't hear of her taking a taxi. He had brought her, and he was taking her home; she had to accept that. They said good-night to their hosts and inside five minutes were on their way in the big, sleek car.

When they pulled up outside the flat he said abruptly, "Ask me in."

Nicola shook her head. "My flatmate wouldn't like it."

He looked at her hard. "Is that the truth, or are you making excuses?"

"It's the truth."

He caught her shoulders as she made a move toward the car door, and twisted her to face him. "Tell me the truth about this, then," he said. "How much did that fiancé of yours really mean to you?"

Angrily, she pulled against his hold. Didn't he know that it hurt her to think about Robin, that she didn't want to talk about that?

"Tell me," Jethro said, his hands gripping her tightly. "Why?"

"I want to know."

Resentment flared. But he wasn't letting her go until he had an answer. "Robin and I were going to be married! I loved him," she said. "It . . . still hurts to think that it's all over, that it's never going to happen."

"But it *is* over, isn't it?" he insisted. "You can't go back to him?"

Nicola flinched. "No, I can't."

"Do you recall," he said slowly, "our last night on board . . . when we kissed?"

She lowered her eyes.

"Do you?" he asked.

"Yes," she answered reluctantly. "Of course."

"Of course," he repeated.

"You know it was nothing," she said. "You shouldn't have . . ."

"Maybe I shouldn't." He paused. "But I did. *We* did. And it was good, wasn't it?"

She stirred restlessly. "Why are you dragging this up? What's the use of having a postmortem on something that happened months ago?"

"That's a point," he said. "So let's try it again, shall we?"

This time he gave her no chance to say no. His mouth met hers with a sureness and skill that she instantly remembered, and almost as instantly responded to. He seemed to check himself for a moment, and then his lips were persuading hers to open, and his hand came to rest on the warm swell of her breast while he kissed her more and more deeply, until she felt dizzy and breathless.

When at last he let her go, she rested her head against him, and with his hand in her hair he said, "It's still good, Nicola, isn't it?"

"I didn't want that," she complained softly, her voice muffled against his shirt. "It wasn't fair."

His lips touched her temple. "You know what they say about love and war."

But it isn't love, she thought sadly. It's loneliness, and a need for comfort, and basic sexual instinct.

She raised her head from his chest and said, "I must go in."

He studied her face as though trying to read her emotions. His arms slipped from her gradually, and his hand lingered on the curve of her neck, his thumb stroking her cheek. Then he opened his door and got out to go round the car and help her onto the pavement.

At the door to the flat he held her arms for a moment and brushed her lips briefly with his. "Goodnight," he said. "See you tomorrow."

Chapter Five

The next day Nicola guardedly answered Jethro's cheerful, "Good morning," with a more subdued one of her own. He stopped by her desk, waiting for her to look up, and when she did he smiled at her and then passed on to his own office without saying anything.

Vivienne looked at her curiously. "What was that all about?"

"I've no idea." Nicola began searching in her desk drawer for a pencil.

"You came to the Seymours' with him last night, didn't you?"

"He said it was business," Nicola explained.

Vivienne made a small, derisive sound. "He fancies you. It's none of my business, but . . . take care, won't you?"

"Do you think I need to?"

"Maybe. Nice and all though he is, Jethro has a

tough core. I've seen it in business, and I wouldn't be surprised if it spills over into his private life."

"I thought you liked him."

"I do, but he's not casting come-hither glances in *my* direction. I wouldn't like to see you hurt."

"I'll take care," Nicola promised.

Claire Carver phoned her at the office on Monday, with an invitation to dinner the following Saturday. "Jethro will bring you," she said.

"I don't know . . ." Nicola began, but Claire added, "I spoke to him a few moments ago, and he said he'd pick you up."

Resigned, Nicola thanked her and put down the phone. Later in the day, just before finishing time, Jethro stopped by her desk. "About Saturday," he said. "I'll call for you at six-thirty, okay?"

Nicola nodded. "Thank you." She looked down again at the work on the desk before her, and after a moment he went away.

The dinner party was a small one, and Nicola was pleased to see Jess and Gareth Seymour again, and Claire's stepfather, who had brought Vivienne.

The conversation at the table was lively, and naturally turned to the subject of Jess's book.

"The reviews aren't bad, are they?" Gareth asked Jethro.

"Most of them seem to have been quite kind," Jess said, "even the patronising ones."

"They're good reviews, for a new writer," Jethro told her. "The book's doing all right in the sales field too. The bookshops say it's moving off the shelves quite fast. We'll have to start thinking about a second edition. And how's the new one coming along?"

"Slave driver. I'm still in the research stage. I only have half an idea for a story as yet."

"The gold-rush background sounds interesting, though," Vivienne interjected. "I'm sure the story will jell eventually. I'm looking forward to seeing the outline, when you're ready."

"So am I," Jethro said. "It'd be nice not to lose the momentum of the first book. Unless a writer's first is a best seller, the public unfortunately forgets the name, and then you're faced with the work of building a modest reputation all over again. So best not to take too long coming up with the next."

Jess grimaced. "Nicola," she said, "you work for this man. Is he this pushy at the office?"

"Worse," Nicola assured her promptly, earning herself a half-humourous, half-threatening glance from Jethro.

Turning to Jess, he said, "Sorry, I didn't mean to be pushy. I'm looking at the realities of the marketplace, but our job is publishing good books, well-written ones. I wouldn't want you to skimp on the job because you felt obliged to produce within a certain time. It would just be nice if we were able to bring out the second book while the public still remembers the first. Some writers do nothing for months after they finish a book, and maybe they need that break in order to put their best into the next one. Unfortunately, it doesn't help to sell their books."

"On the other hand," Vivienne said, "there are those who are so prolific that their work is cheapened. But don't worry about it, Jess. It's Jethro's job to be concerned about the sales. Mine is to oversee the quality of the books, and I don't want you to feel pressured."

"Neither, in fact, do I," Jethro protested mildly. "I was simply stating the facts of the market."

When they had moved into the lounge for coffee, Jethro came to sit beside Nicola on one of the sofas.

Stirring sugar into his cup, he said softly, "I'll get you later for that crack."

Nicola slanted him a glance, saw him looking at her with a gleam of laughter, and smiled back. "I'm terrified," she said lightly.

"So you ought to be." His answering grin was wolfish, and she laughed aloud, but her pulse rate increased, and she turned away from him, looking across the room to where Pietro was bent close to Vivienne, apparently hanging on her every word.

"You like him, don't you?" Jethro asked her.

"Pietro?" Nicola said. "He's very charming." Mischievously, she added, "Every woman's dream. He drops compliments like rose petals in his wake."

"Is that what every woman wants?"

Nicola shook her head. "Only from some men. With Pietro, it's part of his personality."

Gareth claimed her attention then, with a teasing remark about an opinion she had passed at dinner on a recent best seller. Soon they were involved in an amicable argument. Gareth moved his chair closer, and after a while Jethro got up and strolled over to talk to Claire.

Driving Nicola home later, he said, "You enjoyed yourself tonight."

"Yes. They were all interesting people, and the dinner was delicious."

"You got on well with Gareth."

"Yes. I like him and Jess very much, don't you?"

"I don't know him well. What were you talking about all that time?"

"Oh, books, history, even politics for a while. He's very knowledgeable about a lot of things."

"I haven't seen you so animated since we parted on the ship."

She cast him a surprised look, but in the darkness his silhouetted profile gave nothing away.

As he drew up outside the flat, he said, "I have two tickets for the ballet next Saturday. Would you come with me? I know you like ballet."

She remembered that they had discussed it on the ship. He hadn't shared her enthusiasm for the classical ballets, preferring something in a more modern idiom that he termed less artificial.

As she hesitated, he said with a hint of impatience, "Well, will you come with me?"

Nicola took a quick breath and resolutely said, "I'm sorry, but no thank you."

"You have another date?"

She was tempted to say yes. It was the conventional thing to do. But she knew he wouldn't be fobbed off. If he accepted the excuse this time, there would be other invitations forthcoming. Better to make her decision clear and then stick to it. "No," she said calmly, "I don't have a date. I just don't think it's a good idea for us to go out together."

"You went out with me last week, and again tonight."

"Last week you told me it was business. And this week I didn't have much choice. As we were both invited, it would have been silly to refuse a lift."

He didn't reply directly but said, "You enjoyed it, you said so. And you'll enjoy the ballet too." Suddenly changing tack he added, "Please come, Nicola."

Sorely tempted, she nevertheless repeated firmly, "No."

"What *is* it with you?" he said, leaning toward her. "Do you *like* sitting around at home moping about your precious Robin? What will you do with yourself? Wash your hair and read his love letters?"

"I don't have any love letters."

"Well, that's *something!*" he said disagreeably, and to her own surprise, Nicola nearly laughed. If she hadn't known better she would have thought he was jealous. As it was, she guessed that he was piqued at his plans being thwarted. He had got used to having things his own way, and opposition didn't suit him.

"Was that all?" she asked him, deciding to cut the interview short.

He looked almost disbelieving as she fumbled for the door handle. "No, it wasn't!" he snapped.

She half turned her head in surprise, and he suddenly grasped her shoulders and hauled her toward him. "I told you I'd get you later," he said grimly, and kissed her thoroughly, pressing her head against the seat back, his lips moving insistently against hers.

After an initial fruitless bid for freedom, which he quelled without any trouble at all, she didn't fight him, but concentrated all her energy on not responding. After a while he noticed, and lifted his head, trying to see her eyes in the darkness. "Kiss me, Nicola," he said.

Silently, she shook her head.

"What's the matter?" His hand touched her cheek, his thumb caressing her mouth coaxingly.

She moved her head sharply away from his touch. *"Why?"* he said. "I'm not exactly repulsive to you, am I? Not on the evidence of last time I kissed you."

She looked away, then said stoically, "That's exactly why. I don't want to get . . . involved."

"You're scared."

"All right," she said, sounding indifferent. "If that's what you want to think."

"I don't know what to think, do I?" he said irritably.

"You've locked yourself away, retreated into some dark corner of your mind, and all you want to do is stay there. You won't even make an effort to get out and have any sort of a good time unless it's made practically impossible for you to refuse an invitation. You'd rather stay in a bleak little prison of your own making. Well, I won't let you." His eyes narrowed. "I've figured out why it's just me that you're trying to keep out. Gareth Seymour is married, and Pietro Benotti is too old for you, anyway. But I'm a threat to you, aren't I? I might just make you feel something again, and that's what you're afraid of. You'd rather be emotionally dead."

"Even if that were true, it's none of your business."

"I'm making it my business."

What on earth for?

He paused. "Let's just say I feel responsible for you, because you're a member of my staff and I don't like to see my staff unhappy."

"I'm not unhappy."

Rather gently, he said, "I wish *that* were true. You are, but I won't let you wallow in it."

"I am not wallowing! I just don't want to fall from the frying pan into the fire!"

His breath hissed in between his teeth. "Well, that's an admission," he said.

Nicola bit her lip. It was, and she shouldn't have made it.

Fortunately, he didn't seem in a hurry to follow it up. Almost hesitantly he said, "Nicola, if I swear not to lay a finger on you . . . will you change your mind about the ballet?"

Suddenly she was tired of fighting him. After a moment she nodded, and he let out an exaggerated sigh of relief and sat back in his seat. "I'll pick you up," he promised. "Why couldn't you have said yes in the first place?"

He was as good as his word. On Saturday evening he might almost have been the undemanding companion of the cruise. He even made her laugh once or twice during the supper they ate after the ballet. When he drove her home he saw her to the door, but didn't even touch her arm as they went up the steps. She turned to thank him, and he took her hand as he had the first time he kissed her, and looked at her with an air of quizzical enquiry that made her laugh. "I've enjoyed myself," she said. "Thank you."

He still held her hand. She felt the tensile strength of the fingers fastened about hers, caught a whiff of his masculine scent as he bent his head a little closer.

"Thank *you*," he said. "Perhaps we can do it again, sometime."

Nicola, summoning up some willpower, shook her head faintly. "I don't think so."

"Why not?" he murmured, retaining his grip as she experimentally moved her fingers in his.

"I need a breathing space," she said frankly. "Please, Jethro, don't push me."

After a moment he said, "Okay. If that's what you want."

His lips brushed her cheek, and she fought a desire to turn her mouth to his. He released her hand and stepped back, then ran down the steps as she went inside. She went to bed feeling contented and pleasantly tired, and for the first time in months slept soundly without waking in the early hours of the morning to anguished thoughts of Robin.

Her flatmate changed her job, and shortly afterward told Nicola that she was making more money now and could afford to keep the flat on her own. "It isn't that I don't like you," she said, "but I really would prefer to have the place to myself. There's no hurry, but if you could look around for somewhere else . . . ?"

"All right," Nicola agreed, resigned. She couldn't very well stay where she was not wanted, but it was a nuisance. Finding somewhere else to live wasn't going to be easy. She had been lucky the first time. When she mentioned the problem at work, Vivienne put down the blue pencil she was using and said, "I don't know how you feel about living *and* working with a person, but there's room in my house for another one."

"That's awfully kind of you," Nicola said gratefully, "but it isn't urgent. She said to take my time."

"I'm not just being charitable," Vivienne said. "I used to have a friend sharing with me, until she got married last year. I've missed the company a bit, but I don't want to have just anyone living in my home. I decided to wait and make sure I found a compatible person. We fit in well here in the office . . . but it's up to you. Come and have a look, if you like. There's a big bedroom that you could have to yourself, with a couple of armchairs so that you can entertain your own friends in private, and you're welcome to share my sitting room the rest of the time. Plus the bathroom and kitchen, of course."

It sounded ideal, and after going to have a look at the place and finding it even better than Vivienne's description, Nicola moved in the following weekend. The house was an old Paddington villa, and Vivienne had furnished it in a mixture of antique and newer styles. Modern unstained wood tables and chairs sat beside a Victorian book cabinet and a brocade slipper chair, and cream lace curtains flanked a window in front of which stood a long sofa covered in petal-soft cream leather and piled with pastel-coloured silk cushions.

Nicola's room held a queen-sized bed with a bamboo lattice headboard, and two cushioned cane chairs as well as a natural wood dressing table and a big old-fashioned wardrobe with an oval mirror set into the door. The sun struck through the large windows in the morning, and in the evening a tree outside on the lawn threw a cool shadow across the patterned oriental-style rug that covered the floor. In only a few days Nicola felt quite at home. "I love it," she told Vivienne on Saturday, as they shared a drink to celebrate her first week in the house. "Thank you so much for letting me come here."

Vivienne laughed. "I told you, I can do with the company. Not that I expect you to be here all the time, or with me every minute that you're home. But, though I hate to admit this, there are times when I'm slightly nervous of living alone. It's good to have someone else in the place." She raised her glass and said, "Here's to your next week here, and many more to come."

A little later she said, "Do you have a date tonight, Nicola?"

Nicola shook her head. "No, why?"

"It's such a lovely afternoon, and it's obviously going to be one of those balmy Sydney evenings. Why don't we light the barbecue and have steak and salad on the patio, instead of slaving in that hot kitchen to make ourselves a meal?"

"Sounds lovely," Nicola agreed. Just outside the kitchen there was a small brick-paved area surrounded by hibiscus, scarlet bottlebrush and thin, graceful bamboo, with a built-in brick barbecue in one corner.

Vivenne smiled and finished her drink. "I'll get the steaks out now and let them thaw. I've got a packet of four that I've been saving, so do you think you could eat two?"

The smoky aroma of steak on the grill wafted into the kitchen as Vivienne tended the barbecue while Nicola tossed a green salad. When the doorbell rang she called to Vivienne, who said, "See who it is, there's a love! I'm not expecting anyone."

Jethro stood on the doorstep, his eyebrows going up in surprise as he cast a quick glance over Nicola's brief shorts and casual cotton top, and her hair tied back in a ponytail. "Hello," he said. "What are you doing here?"

"I live here now."

"You didn't tell me."

"Should I have?"

He didn't answer that, but looked at her frowningly. "Is Vivienne at home?"

"Out on the patio, barbecuing. You'd better come through."

She led the way, and when he went down the steps to where Vivienne was turning the steaks, she heard him say, "Hello, having a party?"

"Just the two of us, unless you'd care to stay and join us? There's plenty of steak."

Nicola had picked up a salad fork, and her hand stilled, poised above the bowl as she awaited his reply.

He seemed to hesitate a moment; then she heard him say, "I'd like to, if you're sure it's all right."

"Of course it is. I don't issue invitations if I don't mean them. Is this a social call, or business?"

"Well, it was business, really, about those page proofs you were waiting for. . . ."

Nicola had stopped listening. The salad fork idle in her hand, she stared down at the lettuce, cucumber and tomato in the bowl in front of her, feeling oddly dismayed. She could hear him still talking to Vivienne; then he came to the kitchen door. "Vivienne asked me to open the wine," he said. "Where is it?"

She handed him the bottle and the corkscrew, finished tossing the salad, and took it and a basket of sliced French bread out to the round wrought-iron table on the little patio, where cutlery and plates were already set. Vivienne glanced over and said, "Looks good. The steak's ready. I'm glad Jethro arrived. I really don't think I could manage two of these."

"Me neither," Nicola admitted, looking at the thick, well-browned slices of meat. "I've made garlic butter," she added. "I'll bring it out."

Jethro, holding the opened wine, appeared in the doorway as she ran up the steps. Smiling, he stepped aside, but not far enough. As she passed him her bare arm brushed against the knuckles of the hand holding the wine bottle.

She picked up the little pottery bowl of garlic butter, and the salt and pepper shakers. Jethro was still standing by the doorway, watching her. "You look like a kid with your hair like that," he said, "and no make-up."

She said shortly, "We weren't expecting company. I know I look a mess."

"I didn't say that . . . and I didn't mean it, either. I just find it . . . inhibiting." He inclined his head, indicating that she should precede him out the door.

Reluctant to come so close to him again, Nicola hung back. His brows rose questioningly, and then he said, "I don't bite little girls."

Casting him a scornful look, Nicola swept past him, careful this time to not come within touching distance.

He followed her and put the bottle on the table, asking Vivienne, "Any glasses?"

"I'll get them," Vivienne replied, bringing the steaks to the table. "Won't be a minute."

"We need an extra place for you," Nicola said to Jethro. She turned quickly to get cutlery and a plate from the kitchen, glad of the excuse not to be alone with him.

Vivienne came out of the dining room with three glasses from the china cabinet, and they joined Jethro at the table. He waited for them and seated them first. Vivienne smiled at him, but Nicola kept her eyes on the table as she murmured, "Thank you."

She let the other two do nearly all the talking, and later volunteered to make coffee. When she brought out the three cups on a tray, dusk was just beginning to fall, and Jethro, his chair tilted back on its rear legs, was talking quietly while Vivienne sat with her elbows on the table and her hands cupping her face.

Jethro let his chair down as Nicola put the tray on the table. "Smells good," he commented. "Thanks for a fantastic meal, both of you."

As she resumed her seat, Nicola said, "Thank Vivienne. She asked you to stay."

He looked up sharply from spooning sugar into his cup. "Does that mean you didn't second it?"

She said, "It's Vivienne's home. She does the inviting. Anyway, two of us couldn't have eaten all that steak."

"It's your home too, now," Vivienne said firmly, covering a small, uncomfortable silence. "If *you* want to invite anyone, Nicola, please feel free."

Nicola smiled her thanks, but said, "I don't know many people in Sydney."

"Why not?" Jethro asked.

Nonplussed, Nicola looked at him warily. "Well . . . I just don't. I haven't been here very long, after all."

"Long enough," he said curtly. "You don't go out much, do you? Perhaps if you made the effort . . ."

"I don't want to!"

He looked at her with satire in the set of his mouth. "Yes, that's it, isn't it? You've been in this city for months now, you're an attractive, intelligent young woman, and you've made no effort at all to take part in any social life. You don't even have a date for Saturday night!"

"Neither do you, apparently!" she shot back.

Vivienne laughed. "Hoist with your own petard there, Jethro."

His expression lost its gritty look, and he shrugged and smiled. "True. Look at her, Viv. You wouldn't expect her to have such a sassy tongue, would you? You'd think she was fifteen years old, and butter wouldn't melt in her sweet little mouth."

"Oh, stop being so patronising!" Nicola snapped. "And sexist with it!"

Jethro grinned back at her, tipping his chair again as he looked at her flushed face with apparent satisfaction.

Nicola pushed back her chair and got up, leaving her coffee half finished. "I'll start on the dishes," she said in a strangled voice.

She heard the scrape of his chair, and then Vivienne's voice saying, "Jethro, what are you playing at?" as she fled up the steps.

His answer was inaudible, delivered under his breath, and he didn't come after her.

She let hot water into the sink and quickly washed the plates and cutlery that were stacked in it. She had picked up a tea towel, ready to dry, when the other two came in and Vivienne said, "Don't do them all by yourself, Nicola."

"You can do the cups," Nicola suggested, but Jethro plucked the towel from her hand and said, "Guest's privilege, I think. I'll help Nicola, Vivienne. Why don't you go and sit down after labouring over that hot barbecue?"

"I did sit down," Vivienne reminded him, "while we ate."

He cast her a pained look and said, "Viv, dear, I would like a few minutes alone with Nicola." As Vivienne looked doubtfully at him, he added, "I don't like apologising in front of other people."

Vivienne laughed, shrugged, and went through to the lounge. Stiffly, Nicola said, "You don't have to apologise."

"Yes, I do. I was trying to get under your skin, and I guess I succeeded, too. But it was a cheap way of doing it. I'm sorry, Nicola. Believe me."

Surprised, she stood in silence, one hand on the sink counter, her eyes fixed on the floor. Her voice muffled, she said, "It's all right."

He sighed. "It isn't, of course. I always seem to go about things the wrong way with you. It's just that . . . I can't stand the way you retreat into yourself, trying to hide from life."

"I don't!"

"From me, then. Okay, so you got hurt and you don't want to risk yourself again. You've locked up your heart and put a 'NO TRESPASSING' sign on it. You're nervous that I might actually get through to you, and you're making it as hard as you can. Actually, if it wasn't so annoying, I'd be flattered."

She finally raised her eyes. "What does it matter to you?"

His look was calculating, his mouth taking on a familiar sardonic curve, and she thought he was going to say something cutting. "You just don't want to face it, do you? I must be mad."

"One of us is," she agreed. It seemed a logical explanation for this conversation.

He gave a crack of laughter. His hands descended on her shoulders and pulled her closer, his eyes holding hers inescapably. Her heart began a slow, insistent hammering. In an odd voice he said, "You know perfectly well why it matters to me. But you're determined to be blind and deaf to everything except your memories of a man who doesn't even want you!"

"That isn't true!"

Grimly, he said, "Isn't it?" He looked at her consideringly, and then one of his hands came about her shoulders, bringing her even closer, and the other slid onto her nape, holding her so that she couldn't evade the inexorable descent of his mouth onto hers. And then he was kissing her quite fiercely, his mouth parting hers in a passionate invasion, his arm about her tightening until her body was locked to his, until she felt the warmth of his loins through his clothes, against her own bare legs.

Her pulses raced, and a hot, sweet shaft of pleasure ran through her. She shivered with it, and his hand moved from her nape and ran down her spine to its base, pressing her to him. Heat suffused her body, and she wrenched her mouth aside and gasped, "No, Jethro, please, please don't!"

He grabbed at her head as she tried to push away from him. His eyes glittered darkly, and his breathing was uneven. His fingers found the ponytail and held her by it, and she drew in a sharp, sobbing breath as his mouth touched hers again.

Immediately he lifted his head, looking at her searchingly. "What's the matter?" he asked, his voice rough-edged.

"Please," she whispered. "Don't."

Slowly he said, "You really mean it, don't you?" He released her and she twisted quickly, coming up against the sink counter, clinging to it with her hands while she took several deep, steadying breaths.

"But you kissed me back," Jethro said, as though he couldn't understand it.

Nicola shook her head. She really didn't know if she had kissed him back. It seemed to her that he had exerted some overwhelming power over her, that she hadn't had any will of her own, only a body that blindly responded to stimulus . . . the stimulus provided by Jethro's unleashed masculinity.

He took her arm and brought her round to face him. "You did!" he accused her. "Don't deny it now!"

She lifted a hand to ward him off. "I'm not denying it," she said. "I just . . ." She raised pleading eyes to his face. "I'm not ready for this, Jethro."

"No," he conceded reluctantly. "I know you're not." His mouth twisted wryly. "I've been telling myself to back off and give you time. It caught me off balance, finding you here today. I couldn't resist trying. . . ." He shrugged almost wearily. "You'll just have to live with the fact that I . . . want you."

Nicola touched her lips with her tongue, unable to say anything coherent.

"I do want you, Nicola," he repeated, "and I'm not the type to wait forever. You might as well know it."

"Don't I have any say?" she said, rallying a little.

"Of course." He regarded her thoughtfully. "But your reactions just now were unmistakable."

Huskily, she said, "They were purely physical."

"Maybe. You don't dislike me, do you?"

"Of course not."

"Then why are you so determined to fight it?"

"I told you," she said, "I'm not ready to get involved with anyone just yet. And besides . . ."

"Besides?" he prompted.

"You frighten me," she said. His brows rose in disbelief, and she added quickly, "Not physically, I don't mean that . . . although you're strong. . . . I don't think you'd deliberately hurt any woman."

"Thanks." His tone was dry.

"But you're so . . ."

"So . . . what?"

"Hard," she said. "Almost brutal."

He frowned. "I've never been brutal to you."

"Not to me. To . . . Justine."

The silence stretched. "Justine," he said coldly, "was, as I remember, somewhat 'brutal' to you!"

"That isn't the point."

"No. It isn't. Justine," he added, "has nothing to do with us . . . you and me."

She looked up at him in astonishment. "How can you say that?"

"It's true," he insisted. "That's over, Nicola. I don't even think about Justine anymore. But lately . . . I've been thinking rather a lot about you."

Revulsion crept over her like a chill mist. They were all alike, all of them. Robin, who had thrown her over for a girl he had known for only a few weeks; Carol's boyfriend, who had deserted her for someone else and sent her fleeing back to New Zealand to lick her wounds; Jethro, who could so easily and callously dismiss from his mind the woman he had asked to marry him, whose only crime was that she had been intensely jealous of his love for her, and because of that had lost it.

Nicola said wonderingly, "You're heartless. You just go from one woman to another as though they're flowers in a garden for you to pick, and when you see a new one, you want it, so you throw away the one you already have and trample it underfoot."

"The analogy is pretty," he said, tight-lipped, "but not true. It wasn't like that."

"But it was!" she cried. "How can you cast aside Justine like that, and start to . . . to 'want' me, instead? Do you expect me to believe that you 'want' anything more than a substitute for what you've deliberately thrown away? Justine would have had you back; you said so."

"I didn't want Justine any longer . . . ."

"Exactly! It didn't take much, did it? What would I have to do to make you stop wanting me, once you had me? Not a lot, I should guess. I'm sure I should be thrilled that you've decided to cast your roving eye in my direction, but I can do without that sort of compliment, thanks."

"Nicola, will you listen to me . . . ?"

"No. I've heard all I want to, and it sickens me."

He went white, and grabbed her arm. "Nicola!"

She shook off his hand and said coldly, "I'm going to my room. Vivienne's waiting for you in the lounge."

He let her go then, and she went out of the kitchen without a backward glance, and down the passageway to her own room. A few minutes later she heard the faint murmur of their voices in the lounge, and she switched on her portable radio to drown the sound. Not that she could hear anything they were saying, but she didn't want any reminder that Jethro was still in the house.

Chapter Six

Nicola opened the door one evening to Pietro Benotti. It was a moment before he gave her his dazzling Italian smile and said, "Hello, Nicola. What a nice surprise. Is Vivienne here? We're going to the opera."

"She's dressing," Nicola explained. "I heard her using a hair dryer, so she probably didn't hear the doorbell. Wait in the lounge. I'll tell her you're here."

When she came back into the room with instructions from a slightly flustered Vivienne to give him a drink, he was standing patiently in the centre of the room.

"She won't be long," Nicola assured him. "Would you like a drink?"

"Thank you. May I pour it myself, do you think?" he asked, going to the little antique corner cupboard that held a small range of drinks and glasses. "And what about you?"

"No, thanks." She sat on one of the chairs because he seemed to expect it, and when he had got himself a glass of vodka, he came and seated himself on the sofa facing her.

"Do you go often to the opera?" she asked.

"Not for many years. My wife didn't care for it much. But Italians, you know, we love music, and Puccini, after all, was a countryman. Tonight they perform *Madame Butterfly*. You know it?"

"A little. It's very beautiful."

Vivienne came in, looking extremely elegant in powder blue silk crêpe, and a little flushed with haste. "Sorry. I'm not very late, am I?" she said to Pietro.

"I was too early," he answered courteously, putting his glass on the end table and getting to his feet. His eyes glowed with appreciation as he surveyed her. "I'm sorry if I rushed you. Do you want a drink for yourself before we leave?"

"No, not for me. I see Nicola looked after you all right."

"Beautifully, thank you." He paused, looking from one to the other of the women. "You are leaving your guest alone?"

"I'm not exactly a guest." Nicola smiled.

"She's living here now," Vivienne explained.

Pietro's brows rose, and amusement appeared in his eyes. "Isn't she a little young to be a chaperone?"

Vivienne said, "She's not a chaperone. She's company, that's all. I don't need a chaperone."

He smiled down at her. "No, my dear Vivienne, you don't. And she is very charming company. Goodnight, Nicola," he added as he took Vivienne's arm.

"Goodnight," Nicola echoed, watching them leave. They made a strikingly handsome couple. She wondered idly how often Vivienne saw him.

At Christmas Vivienne was going to spend a few days with her brother and his family in Victoria. "I don't like leaving you here on your own," she said to Nicola. "Look, why don't I phone George and Miriam and tell them to expect an extra guest? You won't mind bunking in with one of the kids . . ."

"You're not to do anything of the kind. I've had an offer to spend the day with someone at Christmas if I want to."

Surprisingly, Bettina Yardley had phoned, asking what Nicola was doing over the holiday and offering hospitality. Perhaps she had felt a little guilty, but Nicola had been coolly polite in her refusal. She really didn't want ever to see Bettina again.

She had dispatched Christmas presents for her family in plenty of time and by Christmas Eve had no more shopping to do. She was glad of that, because the streets were full of last-minute shoppers with harassed expressions, carrying piles of gift-wrapped parcels, and the traffic snarled and roared incessantly along streets that shimmered with heat.

At midday she left the office, and in a nearby snack bar ordered a sandwich and a long glass of crushed fresh pineapple and ice. She found a table and had barely sat down when someone pulled out the chair opposite, and she looked up to see Jethro smiling down at her. "Keep that for me," he said, and went to the counter to return in a few minutes with a bread roll stuffed with meat and salads, a slice of cake and a drink similar to her own.

"You need more than that," he said disapprovingly, glancing at her sandwich as he placed his own plate and glass on the table.

"It's too hot to eat." Nicola picked up her pineapple.

"Next month it will be hotter still. How will you survive?"

"Well, at least the office is air-conditioned. Vivienne said you had that installed after you took over."

"People can't work efficiently when the temperature reaches the nineties, which it does regularly in the summer here."

"So it was a matter of efficiency, not the comfort of the workers?"

"Both. They're inseparable." He bit into his roll and leaned back, studying her across the small table. She hadn't been so close to him since the day he had kissed her in Vivienne's kitchen. Lately he had been treating her with cool impersonality, and she told herself she was glad of that because she couldn't have kept on working for him otherwise. The sneaking disappointment that she felt she dismissed firmly as a natural if not very laudable manifestation of vanity. Likewise the feeling she still had that he watched her a good deal when she wasn't looking. The week before, she had seen him meeting a ravishing redheaded woman on the corner of the block where the office stood, and had walked past her bus stop without realising it, fighting a peculiar hollow feeling in her chest brought on by seeing the woman tuck her hand into the crook of Jethro's arm as they entered the nearby car park. So he had found someone else. . . . It was what she had wanted, wasn't it? But she had not thought that it would hurt.

She wasn't in love with him, and it was crazy to care what he did and with whom. At night sometimes she still dreamed of Robin, aching at the knowledge that he was hers no longer. Jethro had an undeniable sexual magnetism that she noticed every time he came near. But that meant nothing beside a long habit of loving Robin. She couldn't forget him so quickly.

"What are you doing at Christmas?" Jethro asked, cutting into her thoughts.

"I've been invited to go to a friend's," she mumbled, breaking a piece off her sandwich.

"What friend?" he asked skeptically.

"Bettina Yardley," she said without thinking.

His brows rose. "You're spending Christmas with *Bettina Yardley?*"

Nicola sighed. "No," she admitted. "Actually, I turned the invitation down."

"After what she did to you . . . to *us,*" he said, "I should think so."

"Yes, well, it was nice of her to ask, I suppose."

"More likely she hoped to pump you about the latest developments. Not that there are any," he added, somewhat cynically. "Are there?"

Not knowing what she could say to that, Nicola shrugged slightly and shook her head. She picked up her drink again, avoiding his eyes.

"Well," he said after a moment, "what *are* you doing at Christmas?"

"I'm all right," she said vaguely.

"I asked you a question."

"Is it any of your business?"

"Yes. I feel some kind of responsibility for you . . . as your employer . . . and your friend. We were friends once, Nicola."

Fleetingly she looked up and found his eyes on her, their expression unreadable. His voice had gentled to an almost coaxing note. "Vivienne told me she's going away," he said. "So what are you intending to do?"

"Vivienne has no need to worry about me, and neither do you. I intend to spend a restful, very pleasant day. I have a phone call booked to my home in New Zealand, and a fat novel that I've been meaning to read for ages, and I shall treat myself to a very special Christmas dinner."

"On your own?"

"On my own."

"It doesn't sound very exciting."

"Exciting it's not," she agreed, "but I assure you I'll be perfectly happy."

"May I make a suggestion?"

"Be my guest." Suggestions were free, and she couldn't very well stop him. All the same, she was on her guard.

"I hope you might be *my* guest," he said. "Or at least, my mother's. She and her husband have a house up the coast. They're insisting that I come for Christmas, and I'm invited to bring a friend."

"I don't think . . ." Nicola started, but he ignored her and ruthlessly carried on.

"My mother is only recently remarried," he explained. "I don't want to play gooseberry to newly-weds. Taking someone along seems the ideal solution."

"What about . . ." the redhead, she was thinking, and quickly bit her tongue, not wanting him to guess that she had seen them, still less that she cared about it.

"Yes?"

"Nothing. Look, it's kind of you . . ."

"It would be kind of *you.*"

She looked at him skeptically. "There must be dozens of people you could ask."

"I'm asking you. I'm sure you'd enjoy it, and if it were anyone else you'd accept the invitation to see something more of the country, wouldn't you?"

He paused, but she didn't answer.

"Come on, Nicola," he urged. "Stop making me feel like the big bad wolf. Remember the good times we had on the cruise."

"With no strings," she put in swiftly.

"Mm." He looked thoughtful. "All right. No strings, okay?" He put out his hand and briefly covered hers where it lay on the table. "It's a lovely place, a beautiful beach. It's got to be better than spending Christmas on your own. You can place your phone call from there, and my mother will be delighted to have you."

The prospect of Christmas alone was daunting in spite of her protestations to the contrary, and the way he had put it, it seemed pigheaded and ridiculous to keep on refusing.

He picked her up early on Christmas morning and drove across the stolid arch of the Bridge as the sun gave a pale glow to the Opera House roofs and stroked into limpid life the waters of the harbour. The day grew warmer as they sped north, eventually finding the coast and following it, losing sight of the ocean occasionally among suburban gardens planted with banana palms and lemon bottlebrush, but always coming back to the rolling, swelling waves, and the white-spumed breakers of the great Pacific racing headlong for the shore.

On a low headland above one of the seemingly endless beaches Jethro drew up in front of a long, white-painted house with a wide verandah facing the ocean. He helped her out of the car as a woman came hurrying through the front door and down the shallow steps of the verandah, followed at a more leisurely pace by a lanky, balding man.

Jethro greeted his mother with an affectionate hug, shook hands with the man, and turned to bring Nicola forward, his hand on her arm.

"My mother," he said. "And this is Hank Porter, her husband."

Mrs. Porter was small and slight and had obviously been a beauty in her youth, her brown hair still thick and naturally waved, her eyes large and very blue, with long lashes. There was an air of vulnerability about her, signs of past strain about her eyes and mouth when she wasn't smiling. Hank and Jethro both seemed to treat her with great gentleness, even in those few moments of greeting.

Later, when the men were setting the table on the verandah for lunch and Nicola offered to help Mrs. Porter in the kitchen, Nicola felt the same protecive urge in herself. The older woman had made a gourmet meal of roast turkey and vegetables, with a salad, in view of the hot weather, and a cold compote for dessert, but she clucked anxiously over lumps in the gravy and fussed in case the turkey hadn't cooked right through. Nicola found herself murmuring reassuring noises while she cut up tomatoes and chopped chives and mixed a French dressing under her hostess's instruction.

The meal was served with wine, and they ate it in a leisurely fashion, the view over the sea adding to their enjoyment. Mrs. Porter turned pink as Nicola added her praise to the men's lazy appreciation of a good meal, and when everyone had finished, and Nicola insisted on helping with the dishes, Jethro pushed his mother firmly into her chair and said, "Nicola and I will do them. You sit there and enjoy yourself."

She protested some more, but Hank chuckled and said, "Let them, Sylvia. Even doing dishes is a good excuse to be alone when you're young, remember?"

Jethro laughed, and Nicola gathered up some glasses and fled into the house.

When Jethro came in minutes later carrying a pile of cups and saucers, she already had the sink full of soapy water and was busily rattling plates into it.

Jethro began drying, his movements sure and efficient. "You've obviously done this before," Nicola commented.

"It's not the first time," he agreed. "Hank wanted to buy Mother a dishwasher but she wouldn't hear of it.

With only the two of them most of the time, she said it would be a shocking waste of money. I think she feels a dishwasher is a step on the way to decadence and decay. It would make her feel lazy and possibly even redundant."

"There's more to a woman's life than washing dishes!"

"There is indeed. I think perhaps she's just discovering that."

Nicola glanced at him as she carefully placed a wineglass on the drainer. "Did your father die?"

"Last year. But he and my mother had separated some time before that."

"Oh, I'm sorry."

He shrugged.

"How long have your mother and Hank been married?"

"About five months."

"You seem quite pleased about it."

"It's the best thing that's happened to her in a long time."

"It must be nice for her to know that you approve. Sometimes children, even grown up ones, get quite jealous if a parent remarries."

Jethro said forcefully, "Even if I didn't like Hank, which I do, I would never subject my mother to that kind of unforgivable interference in her life."

Surprised at his vehemence, Nicola said, "No, I don't suppose you would. Does she . . . are there other children?"

"No, I was the only one." He polished the wineglass so vigorously that she murmured, "Be careful with that, it's crystal."

He grinned at her. "Don't worry, I won't break it. You have one sister, right?"

"Did I tell you that on the cruise?"

"Mm, hmm."

"Fancy you remembering!"

"I remember a lot," he said, turning away from her to put the glass in the cupboard.

"How come you didn't tell me about your family, then?"

"Maybe you didn't ask. Or maybe I did, and you've forgotten."

"I haven't forgotten. I'm sure you never told me."

"Well, there's not a lot to tell about a one-child family. No interesting squabbles like the one you had with your younger sister, when she tore the hair off your doll and made her bald."

"She didn't do it on purpose," Nicola hastened to say. "Susan was never vindictive. Only she wanted the doll and I wouldn't let go, so she kept pulling at its hair until it just came off. It was partly my fault. If I hadn't been so stubborn, holding on, it wouldn't have happened. It taught me a lesson."

"Not to hold on to what's yours?" He looked at her curiously.

"Not to be so possessive that I'd rather see something spoiled than let it go."

His look was arrested. "Quite a lesson. Is that what happened with Robin?" he asked.

"He wanted out, and there wouldn't have been any point in trying to hold him."

They worked on in silence, and as she drained the water and rinsed the sink, he said, "What time is that call to your family supposed to be?"

"Two-thirty."

"Mother said you can take it in her bedroom. You'll be quite private there."

Hearing her own mother's voice over the line was odd at first, and made her instantly homesick. Her

father and Susan spoke to her briefly, and she assured
each of them that she was fine and happy, loving her
job and having a good time. Then her mother came on
the line again. "I wish you could have come home for
Christmas, though, dear. Are you with Jethro?"

Surprise held her silent for a moment. Then she
realised that it was a logical question. "Yes," she said,
with some constraint. "Actually, we're spending the
day with his mother."

"That's nice. You won't be lonely, then. You haven't
said much in your letters . . . about him, I mean. How
are things going?"

"All right." Nicola struggled to sound happy and
casual.

"Well . . . look after yourself, dear."

"I will. I miss you all, but I'm having lots of fun here.
Give my love to everyone."

There seemed nothing more to say, and the call was
costing a fortune as it was. She sat on the bed afterward
feeling unsettled. Perhaps it had been a mistake, but
she was glad to have heard their voices, anyway, and
her mother had been happy. "The best Christmas
present of the lot," she had said at the outset of the call.

She got up, and smoothed the bedcover. At a tap on
the door, she called, "Come in."

Jethro opened the door, saying, "Everything okay?"

"Yes, they're all fine, having a nice, quiet Christmas,
but they said they miss me, and . . ." Her voice wob-
bled, and she tried to turn away, but he crossed the
room swiftly and took her in his arms, pushing her head
against his shoulder and letting her drop a few tears on
his cream silk shirt. "Better?" he asked as she sniffed
the tears to a stop and eased herself away from him. He
held her lightly as she raised the back of one hand and
wiped at the dampness on her cheeks.

"Yes, thank you," she said. "I'm sorry." She managed a little laugh. "That was stupid."

Jethro shook his head. "No, it wasn't." He bent and kissed the moisture from below her eyes, and then placed his mouth gently on hers. It felt very comforting and very right, and she stood perfectly still in his loose clasp until he lifted his head and smiled at her and said, "Do you mind?"

Nicola shook her head. He was so nice in this mood. It made it hard to remember that at other times he had repelled her with his merciless intolerance.

He put his arm about her shoulders and led her out of the room. "We're opening presents," he said.

"Oh, I brought something for your mother. I'll fetch it from my bag."

She had bought a box of fancy chocolates for her hostess, not very imaginative, but then she hadn't known anything about Mrs. Porter, and chocolates seemed safe. When she handed over the wrapped parcel, the older woman said, "You didn't need to do that!" but she looked delighted, and began passing round the chocolates as the rest of the few parcels under the small tree were opened. There were, to Nicola's surprise, two for her. "We knew Jethro was bringing a guest, and just so you wouldn't feel left out, dear . . ." Sylvia explained. "It's only a little thing."

"It was very kind of you," Nicola said warmly, unwrapping a tiny porcelain vase. "And it's lovely, thank you."

Jethro came and sat beside her as she opened the second parcel, also a small package. It held a jeweller's case, and she snapped up the lid to reveal a slim gold bangle with a delicately engraved pattern on it, set with half a dozen tiny garnets. A small card nestled within the circle of gold had Jethro's signature scrawled on it.

"Put it on," Jethro urged in her ear.

"Jethro, it looks very expensive. I don't think . . ."

"Then don't," he suggested curtly and picked up the bangle, possessing himself of her hand. He pushed the bangle onto her wrist and held it up for his mother to see. "Does it suit her, Mother?"

"Yes, it's lovely." His mother smiled. "You look very doubtful, Nicola."

"I'm not sure I should accept . . ."

Sylvia laughed. "Jethro can afford it, and if it gives him pleasure, why not? I'm sure the days are long gone when the only allowable presents a man could give a girl without compromising her were books and chocolates."

"The days are long gone when a girl could be compromised by a gift at all, surely," Jethro commented. But Nicola still looked doubtful.

"Don't you like it?" Jethro asked her.

"Of course I like it!" Nicola said. "Only . . ." She caught a warning light in his eyes and backed down. "Well, thank you very much. It's beautiful. But I don't have anything for *you*," she added. "I wasn't expecting . . ."

"I know," he said. "You're giving me your company for today, and that's all I want from you . . . at the moment."

"How about a walk down to the beach?" Hank suggested. "You young ones might fancy a swim."

"Sounds good," Jethro said. "Feel like a walk, Nicola?"

Mrs. Porter said, "I think I'll stay here. I may even have a short siesta on the verandah."

Nicola changed in a spare bedroom, pulling on a loose muslin shift over her sleek swimsuit, and walked the short distance to the beach with Jethro and his stepfather. Jethro had put on swim briefs and a shirt

which he left unbuttoned, and he took Nicola's towel
from her to carry with his own flung over one shoulder.
It seemed natural when he casually put the other arm
about her as they strolled along the grass verge of the
road and down to the white sand.

The beach was long and clean, with few trees.
Scattered groups of people lay about on beach towels
or played ball games on the firmer sand above the water
line. There was a notice on the lower dunes warning
swimmers to listen for a shark signal and leave the
water at once if it sounded, and a surf patrolman sat
nearby keeping an eye on the people in the water.

The three of them walked along the beach for a
while, and then Hank said, "I think I'll head back now.
You two take your time. Enjoy yourselves."

As he loped away from them, Jethro said, "I think
'young people' aren't the only ones who like to be
alone. Do you get the feeling he can't stay away from
my mother?"

"I think it's . . . rather nice," Nicola said. "Don't
you?"

"Provided it's not carried to excess."

"Can love be excessive?"

"Yes," Jethro said positively. "Some kinds can."

Nicola stared. "But surely then it isn't love?"

"Maybe. Shall we swim?"

The sea looked inviting, and the patrolled area made
it reasonably safe. In New Zealand sharks were now
seen near the shore more frequently than in the past,
but attacks were rare. The swimmers on Australian
beaches, with their shark nets and warning systems,
seemed much more conscious of the dangers than back
home.

Once in the sea, however, Nicola enjoyed the bois-
terous rush of the breakers and the smooth ride into the
beach on the crest of a wave. She was a good swimmer

and was able to keep up with Jethro until an hour later when they waded into the shallows, panting and tingling with exercise and the invigorating tang of salt water, and collapsed onto their towels.

It was late afternoon, and the sun had lost some of its merciless midday heat, drying their bodies with a gentle warmth that sent Nicola into a doze, her head pillowed on her arms as she lay face down.

She woke to a feeling of being watched, and turned over to see Jethro looking down at her, his head propped on one hand as he supported himself on his elbow. He placed an arm across her, his hand on the sand near her waist. "Have a good sleep?" he asked.

"It was only a nap. Should we be getting back?"

"There's no hurry." He shifted closer, tracing a slightly gritty path with his finger from her wrist to the crook of her elbow. "Do you know you're a very restful person to be with?"

"Because I fall asleep?" she said, smiling. Keep it light, her brain told her guardedly. It was very pleasant lying there in the sun with him, enjoying the lazy admiration in his eyes. But it wasn't exactly safe.

Jethro smiled and shook his head. "You didn't do much sleeping on the cruise," he said. "At least not in my company." His hand almost absently stroked her upper arm, and lightly cupped her shoulder. "But you are restful. I remember thinking, the very first time I saw you, that you were just what the doctor ordered. Easy on the eye." His glance slipped down over her body in the brief swimsuit. "You still are."

Nicola stirred, and his hand went to her throat, holding her. "Don't panic," he said softly. "I'm not going to do anything you don't want."

"I don't want . . . anything, Jethro."

He stroked down to her breast, and she knew he could feel her instinctive physical reaction through the damp fabric. With an effort she kept looking into his eyes.

"Say that again?" he invited, his fingers moving insidiously.

Clamping her teeth against the fiercely pleasurable sensations he was arousing, she said, *"I don't want it."*

As his eyes darkened with angry passion, she whispered, "You promised!"

His lips firmed, and he removed his hand to rest it again on the sand. "So I did." He suddenly flung himself on his back, an arm behind his head. "Top marks for willpower, darling. What is it about me that you find so repulsive?"

"You know I don't find you repulsive."

"Not physically. I've had ample evidence of that," he said coolly. "But something makes you hold back every time. And I don't think that it's simply moral scruples. I haven't even come near to inviting you into my bed . . . or myself into yours."

Deciding to carry the battle into the enemy camp, she said, "But you intend to, don't you?"

He rolled over again so that he could see her. "We haven't progressed that far, yet. Why not take things as they come?"

"And then be accused of teasing when it comes to the point and I say no?"

He smiled. "Perhaps you wouldn't want to say no, after all."

"Grandma, what a big ego you have!" she said dryly.

Jethro laughed. "If I have, you've helped," he said. "Because, in spite of what you *say,* you kiss very nicely when you *are* in the mood."

"It isn't a question of mood," she said tartly.

"What is it a question of, then?" he asked. "You still haven't told me what's so objectionable about me."

Nicola sat up, preparing to stand. "I did tell you. I

know you don't understand . . . probably because it's nothing that you don't share with the great majority of men."

She got to her feet and shook out her towel, turning away from him so that the sand wouldn't fly all over him.

He was on his feet, too. "You've got a chip on your shoulder about men in general, haven't you? Have you decided to get back at all males because of what Robin did to you?"

"Of course not. Maybe I just happen to be disillusioned with all males since that, and since . . . meeting you. I find it objectionable that you can reject one woman and be ready to make love to another within days. Your engagement to Justine was hardly over before you were kissing me!"

"I kissed you once before that."

"Yes," she said, remembering the incident on the last evening of the voyage. "And you shouldn't have. Not while you were engaged to her!"

"Let me get this straight," he said mock-solemnly. "You object to my kissing you while I was engaged to Justine, and you also object to my kissing you while I'm not engaged to Justine? When would it be permissible for me to kiss you, do you think?"

"You know perfectly well what I mean! You could at least have waited for . . . well, for a decent interval."

He threw back his head suddenly and laughed. "I'm not *widowed!*" he pointed out. "What would you call a decent interval, exactly?"

"Oh, I don't know!" she said crossly. "But how can you expect me to take you seriously when you can throw aside your fiancée just like that, and start looking around for someone else straight away?"

"I didn't," he argued. "You were right there."

"Yes, and that's the only reason you picked on me,

isn't it?" she challenged him. "I was the handiest, and you'd had the idea put into your head by that stupid magazine article and Justine's jealousy."

He looked stunned for a moment. "Is that what you think? That I was just using you as a sop, a consolation prize? Nothing could be further from the truth!"

Nicola pulled on her shift over the damp swimsuit. She shook back her hair and regarded him with clear eyes. "I think it's pretty close," she said flatly.

She began to walk up the beach, and he snatched up his towel and came striding after her. "Suppose," he said, "I told you that ever since I kissed you the first time, I'd been thinking about you far more often than an engaged man should think about a woman other than his fiancée? What would you say then?"

"I'd say you owed Justine an apology," she said crisply. "And I'd say that's one of the corniest lines I've ever heard, and that you ought to know better than to expect me to swallow it. You had no right to kiss me like that anyway, and you should never have done it."

"Well, look who's calling the kettle black!" he jeered. "As I remember, you took some little part in that kiss yourself!"

"You took me by surprise," she protested. "I wasn't expecting . . ."

"Actually, *I* wasn't expecting anything quite so . . . memorable, either," he said. "If you hadn't responded the way you did . . ."

"Are you blaming *me?*"

"I'm not blaming anyone, but if you're hurling accusations at me, you might remember the saying about glass houses. So why did you kiss me back?"

"*I* wasn't engaged at the time," she reminded him acidly. "Besides, you *made* me!"

He stopped her with a hand on her wrist, twisting her to face him. With deadly quiet, he said, "You know that if you'd showed the slightest resistance I would have let you go."

She looked at him defiantly, then bit her lip as she looked away again. "Yes, I know," she said, her shoulders drooping. "It was as much my fault as yours. I'm sorry."

He slipped his fingers into hers and went on walking, his grip firm and warm. "Don't be sorry," he said. "I'm not. It's one of the most delightful memories of my life."

"And that's what it should have stayed," she sighed. "A memory."

"Why? Fate decreed otherwise. You walked back into my life . . . and I don't intend to let you walk out again."

A sharp breath of wind from the sea lifted her hair and blew several strands across her eyes. Brushing it back with an impatient hand, she said, with a hint of despair, "What do you *want* of me, Jethro?"

"Don't you know that, yet?" he asked her, half humorously. "I want you to marry me, of course. Will *that* make you take me seriously?"

Chapter Seven

Nicola stopped in her tracks. "*Marry* you?" she repeated in stunned tones.

"Is that so unthinkable?"

"Yes!" she answered baldly. Then, as his mouth thinned and his eyes narrowed unpleasantly, she added hastily, "I never imagined that you had marriage in mind!"

"Only seduction?" he suggested. "You do have a charming opinion of me."

A beach buggy came by on its way to the shore, the crowd of youngsters seated in it casting curious glances at them as they stood tensely staring at each other. The noise of the engine drowned Jethro's words and startled Nicola into moving further onto the verge. "We can't talk here," Jethro said grimly, and took her arm, urging her up the slope towards the house.

When they got there they found Hank and Jethro's

mother in the front lounge overlooking the sea, drinking tea.

Jethro put his arm about Nicola as they came into the room, and staggered her by saying, "Mother, give me a character reference, will you? I've asked this woman to marry me, and she's dithering."

"Jethro!" Nicola exclaimed in appalled tones.

Hank chuckled, and Mrs. Porter said, "Jethro, don't tease. If Nicola accepts you I'm sure I'll be very happy for you, but I refuse to aid and abet. Nicola, sit down, dear, and I'll pour you some tea. And don't let Jethro bulldoze you into anything. He's inclined to be bossy sometimes."

Jethro's brows went up. Then he glanced at Hank with what seemed to be curiosity, but he let Nicola go and then found a chair for himself opposite hers, while his mother filled the two empty cups on the tray before her.

"I hope it's still hot," she said, passing one to Nicola. "I only made it a little while ago, and I put a cosy on the pot."

"It's lovely," Nicola assured her after taking a sip. She began chatting to Mrs. Porter about the beach and the gardens lining the road, and managed to avoid speaking to Jethro again until it was time for them to leave.

He had been driving for some time before he said suddenly, with a slight smile, "I think Hank will be good for my mother. She's gaining a lot of self-confidence. I don't remember her putting me in my place so firmly since I was ten years old."

"It might have done you good if she had."

He grinned, casting her a sidelong glance. "So you think I'm bossy, too."

"You're entitled to be . . . at work."

"All right, point taken." He paused. "I don't think a

proposal of marriage comes under the heading of bulldozing, does it?"

"Telling your family about it before I've had a chance to say yes or no does."

He briefly pursed his lips. "I didn't see it that way."

"You were trying to pressure me."

He sighed sharply. "I simply wanted to tell them."

They were coming up over a headland, the road winding along its summit, so that they looked down on the pale sea, colourless in the fading light.

He swung the wheel and steered the car off the road, then halted it near the cliff edge. For a few seconds he sat staring down at the restless undulations of the ocean far below; then he turned to her and said, "Well, this is your chance. Yes or no?"

She was nettled by the arrogance of his tone; he was far too sure of himself, certain of her acceptance, or he wouldn't have risked telling his mother and Hank that he had proposed. She looked up, meaning to say no, but the expression in his eyes confused her. It was tender and slightly amused and enquiring, and yet behind all that was something much more serious and somehow more vulnerable. She opened her mouth to form the refusal, and instead she said, almost whispering, "Do I have to decide right now?"

Something like a spark leaped into his eyes. He said quite calmly, "Oh, I think so. Don't you?" Then he said, "I'll help you make up your mind."

Instinctively she lifted her mouth as he encircled her with his arms. Her lips parted under his gentle, passionate persuasion, and all her senses leaped into life. The roar of the sea was in her ears, the scent of it mingled with the masculine, musky aroma of Jethro's skin. Her own skin tingled and burned when his hands wandered over her throat, down her bare arm, and pushed her skirt up to caress her legs.

He pressed soft kisses along the line of her throat, then shifted his grip so that she lay across his thighs, one arm holding her while the other hand touched her, stroked, explored, finally coming to cup the warm mound of her breast as he claimed her mouth again.

A starburst exploded behind her closed eyes as she responded to his kiss; her body strained against him, helplessly wanton in its unfulfilled desire. Her emotions were so out of control that she became alarmed and began to struggle, fighting his mouth; he lifted his head, whispered, "It's all right, darling," and gathered her body to his, smoothing her hair until she lay against him quietly, willingly. Then he kissed her eyelids, her cheeks, her upper lip first and then the lower one, and left the imprint of his mouth on the taut skin of her throat before his lips possessed her breast, his hands easing the fabric of her dress down from her shoulders to give him access.

Immediately hot desire kindled and flamed, more intense than ever, and she was caught in a dizzy spiral of sensation, her shaking hands touching his shoulders, his neck, his hair; her head falling back and her lips parting on a sigh, so that when he kissed her mouth again, she had no resistance to the passionate invasion of his tongue.

His hand slipped between her thighs, stroking the smooth inner skin, until she was mindless with delight, and when he at last freed her mouth she clutched at him feverishly, her fingers closing on the material of his shirt as though terrified that he would leave her. His lips fastened on her breast, and she felt her legs part slightly under the gentle, insistent movements of his hand. Then he began a series of delicate, intimate caresses, making her gasp as she was assailed by wave after wave of incredible physical sensation; gradually, skillfully, bringing her closer and closer to the release she craved.

At last she shuddered and sobbed and, as his mouth left her, put her arms about him and cried out against the salty skin of his throat, and then lay perfectly quiet while his arms cradled her and he murmured, "Shh, my beautiful." And then, his lips grazing her cheek, he whispered, "Say yes, darling. Say it." His arms tightened momentarily, and his mouth touched the corner of hers.

She wanted to obey him, but some vestige of sanity remained, cautioning her against it. "You don't play fair, Jethro," she murmured. "I can't . . . I won't give you an answer now."

He went still, then moved sharply, and firmly put her away from him, easing her back into her own seat. She straightened the skirt of her dress, and, suddenly conscious of her dishevelment, she pulled up her bodice and tried to fix her hair, running her tongue over her fevered mouth, as Jethro started the engine.

For the rest of the drive he seemed distracted. Once he leaned over and looked for something in the glove compartment. She asked him what he wanted, and he grunted and said, "A cigarette. I thought there might be a leftover packet in there."

"But you've given up smoking."

He gave her a sidelong grin. "Yes. But right now I could do with one."

She knew why, and her cheeks burned. The house was in darkness when he drew up outside it at last, and as she fumbled with the key at the front door he took it from her and inserted it in the lock. He swung the door open and asked, "Do you want me to check the place over before I leave?"

"No, it's all right," she said. "Everything was locked."

He caught her hand in a light clasp as she passed him to go in, and she said, "Would you like some coffee?"

"No," he said. "Tempting though the offer is, I'll pass tonight."

She felt incredibly tired, too tired to think. He looked down at her bent head, and lifted it with a hand under her chin. "Your eyes look enormous," he said. "I know what they mean by that expression about drowning in a woman's eyes."

He kissed her lightly, lingeringly, not putting his arms about her, and then gave her a little push inside and said, "Lock the door. I'll come round tomorrow morning."

In the cold light of morning she recalled the previous day's events with something like disbelief. Jethro couldn't have asked her to marry him . . . but he had. She couldn't have responded to his caresses in that blind, headlong way . . . but she had. She showered and dressed quickly, in a pale pink shirt-style blouse and grey cotton skirt, remembering that he had promised to call.

By the time he rang the doorbell she seemed to have been up for hours with nothing to do but think and become increasingly, ridiculously nervous.

When she opened the door to him, he smiled at her and bent to kiss her, but she moved her head aside so that his lips only grazed her cheek. He closed the door with a deliberate movement, and a frown appeared between his dark brows. He reached for her, his hands imprisoning her shoulders, and waited for her to look at him, then kissed her again, this time unerringly finding her mouth, exploring it with an irresistible finesse, until the familiar warmth of desire invaded her, and she kissed him back.

There was a glint in his eyes when he finally released her, a satisfied curve to his mouth as he murmured, "That's better," rousing in her a slight antagonism.

She turned away from him and led the way into the sitting room, her movements seeming jerky and unco-ordinated. "Would you like a drink?" she asked him, gesturing towards the corner cupboard.

"A bit early in the day, I think," he answered.

As she made to sit on one of the chairs, he captured her hand in his and led her instead over to the long sofa, bringing her down on it to sit close to him, his arm going about her shoulders. "I've got a better idea," he said suggestively, his free hand going purposefully to the top button of her blouse.

Nicola swiftly caught his fingers, as she shook her head and said, "No."

Jethro smiled, lifting her hand in his. He kissed her fingers, and then took the tip of one into his mouth, closing his teeth on it gently, while his tongue played around it erotically.

Flushing under his merciless eyes as they watched for her reaction, Nicola bit hard on her lower lip and dropped her eyes to where her other hand was curled in her lap. When Jethro removed her finger from his mouth and turned his attention to the next one, she suddenly pulled sharply away and stood up.

His eyes narrowed, his arm resting along the back of the sofa, he asked, "What's the matter?"

"Nothing. It's . . . it's a bit early in the day for that, too."

Jethro got to his feet, laughing. "Do you think so? Okay, what do you suggest we do, then?"

Nicola shrugged uneasily. "I don't know. Shouldn't we talk?"

"What about?" He surveyed her rather critically. "Our wedding date?"

Her eyes darted to his face and away again. "You're taking a lot for granted."

"Are you turning me down?"

"I think we should get to know each other a whole lot better."

"What a good idea," he said softly, coming toward her.

"Not in that way," she hastened to say.

He smiled, but something in his eyes made her uneasy. "Okay," he said, "but come and sit down, anyway. If you want to talk, let's be comfortable."

He brought her with him back to the sofa, and sat with his arm about her, his fingers gently stroking her arm. "Don't you think," he started, "we know each other quite well? I know what you like to eat, how you drink your coffee, what books you enjoy, what form of entertainment you prefer . . . I even know something about your childhood, and your family. I know that you're rather reserved with new acquaintances but fun when you open up, and that you're loyal to a fault, and scrupulous about treading on other people's territory. And stubborn, and passionate, but you can be very strong-minded about that. You're even-tempered, and don't parade your emotions, but you won't allow anyone to bully you. When I've tried, you've given me short shrift. What do you know about me?"

"Quite a lot, I suppose, on the surface," she said slowly. "Likes, dislikes, but that's not important."

"You don't think so? Similar interests aren't important?"

"Yes, they are, but as long as each partner tolerates the other's interests, I don't think that they need to share everything."

He nodded. "Okay. I'll go along with that."

"I know you're good at your work, and you believe in it, that you put a lot of yourself into the business, not just financially, but mentally, even emotionally. But I'm not sure," she went on, "what else involves you emotionally."

"I thought I'd made that clear. *You* do."

She looked away, and his arm tightened about her. He said, "Why does that make you nervous?"

"I'm not nervous. I just don't understand why you want to marry me."

"Did that fool who jilted you destroy all your confidence?" he demanded. "You're lovely and intelligent and restful, when you're not getting jittery over my wanting to make love to you, and I want to be with you, all the days of my life. Isn't that enough?"

"And . . . Justine?" she asked. "It isn't so long since you wanted to marry her."

"She's beautiful, of course, and good company, and we had . . . a certain compatibility in some areas. I thought that was enough. But when I saw you and her together . . . I realised that I didn't really care for Justine at all. She was all claws and spitting insults, and I saw you standing there and taking it with such . . . dignity. And I thought, *I'd rather have her.*"

"Jethro!" She pulled herself out of his arms and stood up, regarding him with appalled eyes. "How could you make a comparison like that? Justine had every right to be angry; you can't judge her in that self-righteous, callous way."

He stood up too. "I can't help it. Her behaviour sickened me. Maybe that's unjust and narrow-minded of me, but I couldn't stand a marriage full of scenes like that. My mother suffered all her life from my father's insane jealousy. He made her life a misery until she left him when she couldn't stand it any longer. That kind of possessive love is an emotional straitjacket, and in the end it kills love in both partners. I hadn't realised that Justine was capable of it. Some men might be flattered to be the object of such . . . passion. But it's not for me. I've seen the destructive side of it in my parents' marriage, and I know I couldn't live with it.

"You were so different. Even that first day, I picked you out because of your . . . serenity. If I allowed myself to think about it, which I didn't in those first weeks when we met, there was always a sexual attraction, but that was a minor factor at first, I suppose because I deliberately suppressed it. Occasionally, though, I got caught unawares. That day you came into my office and I offered you a job, I couldn't help remembering the one time I'd kissed you, and wondering if you remembered it, too."

She had remembered it and, looking at her face, he laughed, knowing what her expression meant. "You did," he said, and reached out his hands to grasp her shoulders. "You do feel something for me, Nicola. I know you don't give your kisses casually. But you've kissed me often . . . and last night, you let me do a lot more." He paused as she hid her face against his shoulder. "Are you still pining for Robin?"

She thought about it for a moment, then shook her head with a sensation of astonishment. Robin was nothing anymore except a vaguely unpleasant memory. She didn't know when it had happened, but the healing was apparently complete at last.

He held her face in his hands, turning it up so that he could search her eyes. "You told me before that you weren't ready," he said. "But how about now?"

"Give me time," she pleaded.

His eyes darkened. "I have."

"Not enough."

"Will it ever be enough?" A slightly calculating look flickered in his eyes. "You're afraid of committing yourself, aren't you?"

"I'm not sure how I feel about you."

"Let's find out," he suggested, and his mouth came down hard on hers.

She made a protesting gesture with her hands, half turning from him, and he caught suddenly at her wrist, pulling her into his arms. His mouth found hers again and parted her lips, her head tipped back against his arm. His other arm held her to him, so that her initial stiff resistance was negated, stopped before it had properly started, his arms, his mouth, his body overwhelming her, keeping her in thrall to him while his lips persuaded, forced, pleaded, until she yielded to him, sighing her surrender into his mouth, going suddenly pliant against him, her back arched over his arm, her thighs between his, her eyes closed in dizzy ecstasy as her mouth clung to his in passionate reciprocation.

He knew when she gave in, and she heard him, felt him, make a low, growling sound of satisfaction in his throat. His lips left hers and made a burning foray down the side of her neck and settled on her shoulder, and he shifted his grip to unbutton her blouse all the way to her waist, and take her breast in his hand. The caress brought a hoarse little cry to her lips, and he stifled it with his mouth as he kissed her again, deeply, his hands moving urgently on her flesh, her flimsy bra pushed aside so that he could feel her responses and tantalise her with his fingers.

Nicola shuddered with pleasure, and he left her mouth again to trail his tongue over her skin, following the path of his hands. She cried out again, and heard him draw in his breath sharply. Then he lifted her in his arms and carried her swiftly from the sitting room into the darkness of the passageway, making for her bedroom. Her arms were locked about his neck, her mouth open against the salt-tasting skin of his throat, her lips feeling the heavy beating of the pulse there, her eyes closed.

She heard him shut the door behind them, then felt the softness of the bed underneath her as he gently lowered her onto the cover. He straightened, and she heard the rustle of his clothing as she shakily whispered his name, turning her head to look at him through half-closed lids.

"I'm here," he said, and then he was beside her, turning her into his arms. Her trembling hands found the warmth and smoothness of his skin, roughened on his chest and arms by crisp hair. "Jethro," she said doubtfully, even while her hands fascinatedly explored the textures of his shoulders, his chest, his hard, flat diaphragm, "Jethro, I don't think that we should be doing this . . ."

"We should," he said. "You're going to marry me." His hands were tugging at the belt on her skirt. She felt it give, heard it fall to the floor. He kissed her, a long, drugging kiss, and even as she drowned in the blissful sensations he was giving her, she knew dimly that he was removing her skirt, unhooking the fastening of her bra, doing wonderful things to her with his hands now that they had unrestricted freedom to touch her in every way imaginable.

Her body was almost out of control, wanting him desperately, wanting to give in utterly to sensation, to feeling, to the sheer intoxication of the delicious desire that threatened to swamp her. But her mind still functioned, and her mind was saying wait, wait, he's rushing you; he wants to make you commit yourself; do you know what you're doing?

She moaned, her head moving in negation, and his hands came to her face and held it between them as his mouth came down again on hers. Her "No . . ." was buried in his kiss, her hands pushing ineffectually against his shoulders simply ignored. He grabbed one of them in his and brought it down between them, pressing against his heart, and she experienced again a leaping flame of desire from deep within her. But when he raised his head, she choked out, "Jethro . . . stop."

"Shh." He stroked her hair back from her hot face, dropping tiny kisses along her forehead, on her temple and her cheeks. "You're so beautiful." His hands told her so, too, exploring her body with the touch of a master, sensitising her skin so that it burned under his fingers. She couldn't think straight anymore, with his mouth wandering over her face, his fingers teasing her skin, arousing her even against her conscious will. "Jethro," she pleaded. "Don't. I don't want this. . . ."

He breathed laughter against the skin of her throat, his lips tormenting her. "Darling, that's not true. You want it . . . as much as I do."

"No," she gasped.

"Yes," he said, and kissed her again, stifling her protest, his hands and his mouth combining in sensual coercion. He had done this last night, made her giddy and mindless and so bemused by passion she would almost have agreed to anything. It was a kind of sweet torture by pleasure, deliberately engaged in to get him what he wanted.

Resentment began to fight through the sexual excitement he was creating, and she tried to gather her thoughts, to express them so that he could understand her doubts. But he wouldn't give her a chance. His mouth fastened on her breast, and she closed her eyes tightly and willed herself to some sort of resistance, but even as she pleaded with him, her "No, no, oh please, no . . ." became a sobbing whisper of abandonment. Triumphantly he returned to her mouth, sure now of her capitulation, and Nicola, her resistance spent, began to cry hot tears of humiliation and rage and a kind of pain.

The tears stopped him. He drew away from her, touching the moisture on her cheeks with his fingers, then muttering a curse under his breath. Roughly he said, "Do you mean it? Do you want me to stop?"

Gritting her teeth, because with one part of her she desperately wanted him to stay and finish what he had begun, she finally managed to say clearly, unequivocally, "Yes."

He gave a sharp, frustrated sigh, and rolled off the bed. "All right. You can stop crying. I'm not going to force you."

She fumbled for the bed cover, pulling it over her. She knew he was dressing quickly, and turned her head away from him. He sat on the side of the bed, and she stiffened as she felt his weight on the mattress. His hand touched her shoulder. "It's all right," he repeated. "Can I get you anything? A drink . . . ?"

"No." She took an unsteady breath, controlling herself with an effort. "No, thank you."

The backs of his fingers brushed her cheek, wiping the tears away. "I'm sorry, Nicola," he said soberly. "I didn't mean to upset you."

She felt an urgent desire to turn her cheek against his hand, but she quelled it. "Please go now, Jethro," she murmured.

His hand fell away, and he stood up. "I don't understand," he said. "Why won't you let yourself love me?"

"You can't run your love life the way you do your business," she said. She turned, holding the sheet over her breasts, and stared at him. "You were trying to manoeuvre me."

"What do you mean?"

"I think you know what I mean," she answered. "It won't work, Jethro. If I do say yes to marrying you, it won't be in bed. I want to be in charge of all my faculties when that decision is made. Now please go away."

"When does Vivienne come back?" he asked her.

"Sometime tonight."

"It's not late. How about a trip to the mountains?" As she hesitated, he added, "You said we should get to know each other better."

"All right. But please . . . wait in the other room."

He smiled and left her, closing the door very quietly behind him.

They drove out of Sydney and up to the Blue Mountains, where the air was cooler and the magnificent, rugged sweep of smoke-coloured, bush-covered slopes and valleys viewed from vantage points along the road made her problems seem insignificant. Strolling along a path overhung with spicy-smelling eucalypts and littered with the narrow fallen leaves that crackled under their feet, she accepted Jethro's arm about her waist and replied to his comments on the scenery with a dreamy appreciation of her own.

The path wound upward to a jutting outcrop of rock, and as it got steeper, she said, "You go ahead. I'd like to rest here for a while, and I don't particularly want to climb up there."

"Okay." He watched her find a comfortable spot from which she could see the distant mountains rising against a pale sky, and went forward, stopping to study the rock before climbing up its rugged outline and standing on top, outlined against the distant view and the sky, looking down at a five-thousand-foot drop, only part of which was visible to Nicola. A breeze ruffled his hair and stirred the cotton of his shirt, and

Nicola suddenly recalled with piercing clarity the way he had looked as she glimpsed his naked body before he joined her on the bed earlier on.

She looked away, forcing her gaze to the view, the folds of the valleys and the long steep slopes of the hills seen between the peeling trunks of the eucalypts.

A scraping sound and a thump made her turn again to the rock, but she found it empty. Jethro had disappeared. Sudden fear lurching in her stomach, she shot to her feet, shouting, *"Jethro!"*

In less than a second he appeared round the base of the rock, and she fell back against the trunk of the tree behind her, closing her eyes with relief.

She heard his footsteps bounding down the track toward her, and then his voice saying anxiously, "Nicola? What's the matter? What happened?"

"Nothing," she said, opening her eyes. "You gave me a fright, that's all. One minute you were there on the rock, and the next time I looked you'd disappeared."

Comprehension dawned, and he shook his head and reached for her, pulling her into his arms, his face on her hair. "I didn't do it on purpose," he said. "It's nice to know you care, though."

"Of course I care." She jerked away from him and started walking back to the car. As he got in beside her and slammed the door, she said quite calmly, "I do care, Jethro. I've made up my mind."

He turned slowly to face her, and waited.

Nicola took her bottom lip between her teeth, then released it and said softly, "The answer is yes."

His hand came up and very gently smoothed her hair back from her cheek, then touched her face, her throat, while his eyes gravely studied her. "Thank you, Nicola," he said. His hand moved to cup her head, bringing her closer as his mouth descended with exquisite slowness and settled on hers. He began the kiss almost tentatively, his lips barely touching hers as he explored the outline of her mouth, playing over it teasingly until she raised her hands and put them about his neck. His arms came around her, and his mouth became insistent, probing, then passionately demanding. It was a long, arousing kiss, and when they finally drew apart Nicola's heart was beating heavily, and Jethro's breathing was uneven, his face flushed. He reached out and touched her throat, then lightly ran his hand down over the curves of her body in a possessive, intimate gesture. The sunset was splashing glories of colour across the sky behind the deepening purple of the mountains and shafting vivid golden rays into the car. He picked up a tress of her hair, watching the play of light turning it to gold, then leaned over and kissed her throat, his tongue darting into the hollow at its base, his hand shaping her shoulder, then her breast and her hip.

"We can't stay here," she said huskily, her hand dreamily playing with his hair, her eyes unseeingly on the swaying leaves of the trees about them.

Reluctantly he drew away. "No," he said. "Though I don't see why not."

She smiled at him bemusedly, and he grinned back and started the car. When they reached the highway, he put out his left hand and closed it over her thigh just above her knee, his thumb caressing her skin. He drove nearly all the way like that, while Nicola's head rested against his shoulder.

Chapter Eight

They arrived back in the city quite late, and Jethro suggested a meal before driving her home. She freshened up in the restaurant's ladies' room, and examined her reflection in the mirror with some interest. The day outdoors had brought extra colour to her cheeks and a sparkle to her eyes, and the sun had bleached her hair so that as she combed it the light behind her gave it a soft glow around her face. A touch of lipstick lent her mouth a voluptuous look, and stroked-on shadow imparted extra lustre to her eyes. Recklessly she undid one more button of her blouse, giving the casual outfit a softer, less tailored appearance. She looked good, she thought with slight surprise. The knowledge gave her extra confidence and poise as she reentered the restaurant and made her way back to the table where Jethro waited for her, watching her progress across the room.

His steady scrutiny made her very conscious of the

way her thighs moved under the skirt, the way her belt emphasised her small waist and the blouse outlined the shape of her breasts. As she sat down his gaze seemed to linger on the undone button, and she had difficulty meeting his eyes as they rose, a hint of amusement in them, to hers.

"I've ordered some wine," he said, "but I don't know what you'd like to eat."

The waiter brought the menu, and she chose a fruit cocktail followed by Moreton Bay prawns and squid rings in a rice dish. Jethro ordered a fish entrée and ham steak with pineapple, and then said to her, "A sweet?"

"No, thanks." She shook her head. "I don't often eat sweets, and I'm sure this will be enough for me."

"A cheese board, then," Jethro said to the waiter as the man took the menu card from him. When he had gone, Jethro smiled at Nicola and said, "You're not a sweet girl?"

She grimaced at the double meaning, and said, "Occasionally."

Jethro laughed. "Yes. You're very deceptive."

"Deceptive?"

"Like a marshmallow with an unexpected, tart centre."

"I don't know that I care for that description."

"Well, put it this way. The first time I saw you, I thought you'd be soft and sweet all through."

He didn't elaborate, but the rest was clear. "You've discovered I have a tough streak," she suggested.

"Mm. You're a hard nut to crack."

He had done it, though, and his triumph showed. She looked at him rather ironically. Their wine came, and then their meal, and she kept the conversation light and almost formal. Jethro filled her glass again and again, and she sipped at it and felt pleasantly exhilarated. By the time they left, and Jethro slipped a hand under her arm on their way to the door, she felt she was gliding over the ground rather than walking.

At the house Jethro took her key and pushed open the door, and came with her into the hall.

"Vivienne's home," she said as she closed the door quietly behind him.

"How do you know?"

"Her bedroom door is shut. It was open when we left."

He followed her into the darkened sitting room, switching on the light, so that she blinked in the sudden glare as she turned to face him.

"We'll go shopping at lunchtime tomorrow," he said. "I want to buy you a ring."

"Do we need it?" she asked him.

"Don't you want one?"

"I don't think so." She remembered the huge ruby that Justine had worn on her third finger, and the more modest diamond cluster that Robin had given her. "No," she said firmly. "No ring."

"If you're sure."

"Yes, I'm sure."

He said, "Would Vivienne disapprove if I stayed?"

"She might. I might, too."

He raised his eyebrows, and came over to her, catching her hands in his. "Don't forget you've promised to marry me."

"If it should slip my mind," she said, "remind me."

His eyes glinted with humour and something else. "I will," he said. "Like this."

He kissed her until she was breathless, and then drew her down on the sofa and slid his hand into her blouse while he kissed her again.

Some time later, as he held her across his lap, his hand on her thigh while her cheek lay against his chest, bared by his opened shirt, he said, "I love those little noises you make, but this isn't enough. Marry me soon, Nicola. I want you in my bed every night."

Nicola wriggled out of his arms. "It's late," she said. "We have to work tomorrow."

He looked at her broodingly and stood up. "You're the most exasperatingly evasive woman I've ever known."

"Jethro, I'm tired," she said. "I've only just agreed to marry you. Don't force me to start thinking of wedding dates now."

He laughed. "I should know by now, you hate to be rushed. I'll see you tomorrow, anyway. Goodnight, darling."

She raised her face for a last lingering kiss, and went with him to the door. The note of the car engine came faintly to her ears as she made her way slowly to her bedroom and let herself fall on the bed. The darkness seemed to echo with the sound of his voice; her body still throbbed with the aftermath of his lovemaking. The imprint of his hands was on her flesh, and her lips were hot and swollen from his kisses. She should get up and go to the bathroom, take off her makeup and change into a nightgown. She lay there thinking about it for a while, then drifted into sleep.

She didn't mention the events of the last two days to Vivienne, but after they arrived at the office, she had been sitting at her desk for only a few minutes when Jethro came in, said, "Good morning, Viv. Hello, darling," and, leaning on the back of Nicola's chair, dropped a kiss on her cheek.

Vivienne blinked, trying not to look astonished, and

Jethro laughed and said, "She hasn't told you, has she?"

"Told me what?"

"We're getting married," Jethro explained.

"You are?" Vivienne dropped the pen she had been holding in her hand. "Well . . . congratulations. I hope you'll be very happy."

"Thank you. You're the first to know." He propped himself against Nicola's desk, facing her, and said, "I thought you'd have broken the news to Vivienne."

"When is it to be?" Vivienne asked.

"We don't know yet," Nicola said at the same time that Jethro answered firmly, "Very soon. Within a few weeks."

Vivienne laughed and said dryly, "I see."

Jethro swung his head to look at her and said, "You do, do you?"

Vivienne raised her hands in a gesture of peace. "I'll leave you two to work it out," she said. "Excuse me, I have to see someone in Dispatch."

"Vivienne," Nicola said urgently. "Don't tell anyone else yet, please."

Jethro raised his brows, but Vivienne nodded. "Okay."

When she had gone, Jethro regarded Nicola with a slightly grim and questioning look, and she said, "I haven't even told my family."

"So . . . tell them now." He suddenly got up, hauling her to her feet and pressing a swift kiss on her lips. "What's the number?"

"You're going to phone them? Now?"

"Yes," he said. "They'll be up, won't they?"

Calculating the time difference, she said, "Yes, just."

"Come on, then. What's the number?"

She gave it to him, and within minutes he had her mother on the line, was telling her his name, saying,

"Nicola has something to tell you," and handing her the receiver.

"Mum?" She hesitated. Jethro's arm came about her shoulders; his face was only inches from the receiver as he listened to her mother's voice. "Jethro said you have some news."

"Yes," she said, her mouth suddenly dry. "I'm . . . we're getting married."

"Nicky, that's wonderful! Are you happy? Well, of course you are! When can we meet him? When is it to be?"

Jethro took the receiver and said firmly, "Will three weeks give you enough time to organise a small wedding, Mrs. Grey? Or could you come over, if we have it in Sydney?"

"Three weeks!" Mrs. Grey yelped. "I don't know . . . I think so. We'll try."

Nicola retrieved the phone and said, "Don't worry; it doesn't have to be so soon. We haven't really decided on a date yet. When we do," she added, looking at Jethro, "I'll write."

"But you will come home to be married, won't you, dear?" her mother asked anxiously.

"I expect so. We'll talk about it." She exchanged a few more remarks before ringing off and turned immediately on Jethro.

"You've got to stop doing that!" she told him, folding her arms as she leaned on the desk.

"Doing what?" He stood with his hands casually thrust into his pockets, his eyes watchfully amused.

"Manipulating me! You only rang my mother so that you could pin me down to a date."

"What a nasty, suspicious mind you have," he mocked her.

"And what a devious one you have!" she retorted. "I'm beginning to understand how it works."

"Do you think so?" He shook his head. "I doubt it. What's wrong with getting married in three weeks' time?"

"Supposing I wanted a big wedding with all the trimmings?" she demanded.

"Do you?"

"No."

"Well, then." He smiled with consummate charm. "What's the problem?"

"I might want to get married at home, though."

He shrugged. "Fine. I know your family means a lot to you."

"Have you told *your* mother?"

"I'd like to be able to give her a date."

Nicola shook her head. "Not now, Jethro."

"Okay." He seemed to give in quite easily. "We'll go to my place after work and talk about it."

In his apartment he poured champagne for them both, and toasted her as they sat on the couch, his arm resting casually behind her. When she put down her empty glass, he followed suit, and turned her to face him with his fingers on her cheek, and kissed her with a great deal of gentleness. "It's okay," he reassured her softly when she stirred uneasily in his arms. "I realise you don't want to be rushed, darling." He kissed her again, then shifted so that her back was against his chest, his arms encircling her as he half reclined on the cushions. His mouth nuzzled her neck, her cheek, the hollow beneath her ear. "Comfortable?" he murmured.

Nicola nodded. She was very comfortable, tingling with a pleasant sensation. After a while he stopped kissing her and said, "Where would you like to live?"

"Mmm?"

"Where do you want to live?" he asked. "After we're married."

"I·hadn't thought about it."

"You've hardly thought about being married to me at all, have you?"

"Give me a chance, Jethro!" She struggled out of his hold and sat up. "I haven't got used to the idea, that's all."

"Come back here!" he growled, catching her again in his arms and hauling her against his chest. "And don't be so touchy, woman."

"Well, don't you be so impatient!"

He laughed, and turned her so that she half lay on the sofa. He smiled down at her flushed face and said, "I want you. I want you in my home, in my bed. You'd better get used to that idea pretty damn quick!" He kissed her lingeringly, until her arms went round his neck, her breath coming faster as his lips lazily moved over hers. When he raised his head he said softly, "Soon, Nicola. Don't keep me waiting too long. I need a day . . . a date."

What reason was there to wait, after all? She knew her mother would like her to be married at home, but a small wedding with only her family and his mother and stepfather and a few friends wouldn't take long to organise.

. "Three weeks," she said, and saw his smile of triumph before he bent again to her mouth. Releasing her, he said, "You just have to assert your independence, don't you?"

She heard almost the same words as she let herself into the house that night, her lips still warm from Jethro's final good-night kiss.

Pietro was in the lounge with Vivienne, saying in

exasperated tones, his accent more marked than she had ever noticed, "Why do you fight me like this? You must always assert your independence!"

"I don't want to fight you, Pietro," Vivienne's voice said firmly. "But I wish you would try to understand . . ."

"Understand?" His voice rising, Pietro said, "What man can ever understand a woman!"

Nicola started forward. Obviously this was a private conversation, and they had been too absorbed to hear her come in. The door of the room was open, and she didn't think she could get past it without their seeing her. It was better to make her presence known.

Vivienne was saying tartly, "Some at least make the effort. You're so rooted in nineteenth-century Italian tradition you don't even—"

Nicola stopped in the doorway as Vivienne broke off, paused for a surprised moment, and then said lamely, "Oh, hello, Nicola." Her face was a little flushed, and her eyes unusually bright. She was standing in front of one of the chairs as though she had just jumped up from it, and Pietro, his mouth grim and his black eyes flashing with temper, was standing too, one hand thrust into his trouser pocket, his shoulders aggressively forward.

"Sorry—am I interrupting?" Nicola glanced ruefully from one to the other. "I'm off to bed now, anyway. Good-night."

"It's all right, you don't need to go," Vivienne said, and at the same time Pietro said, "No, no, don't go, Nicola. Perhaps *you* can explain to me about women, whom it appears I do not understand!"

Nicola shook her head, and he came forward to grasp her elbow and propel her into the room. She said, "That's a tall order, Pietro. I don't think I can . . ."

Vivienne said crisply, "It isn't fair to drag Nicola into our quarrel, Pietro. Leave her alone."

He turned on her, his eyes angry, before visibly controlling himself. Nicola felt his fingers tighten quite painfully on her arm; then he released her and said, "No, you are right, of course. I apologise, Nicola." He paused, then smiled at her and said, "And I believe I must felicitate you on your coming marriage. May I wish you every happiness?"

"Thank you."

Vivienne said, "How about coffee all round?"

Nicola shook her head, and Pietro said, "No, not for me. I think I have outstayed my welcome. Is it not so, Vivienne?"

"It is not so!" Vivienne said. "But I don't think there's any sense in continuing this discussion tonight. Perhaps we should both sleep on it."

"Perhaps." He went over to her and with a hand lightly on her shoulder, kissed her mouth. "Goodnight," he said. "I will let myself out. Goodnight, Nicola."

Catching Nicola's enquiring glance as they listened to the controlled slam of the front door, Vivienne coloured a little. "Change your mind about that coffee?" she suggested.

"Yes, all right." Nicola followed her through to the kitchen, getting cups from the cupboard as Vivienne put coffee grounds into the percolator. She had thought that Vivienne wanted to talk, but it was not until they were both seated at the little kitchen table with steaming cups in their hands that the older woman sighed and said, "I suppose you're wondering what on earth that was all about?"

"Sort of," Nicola admitted. "But you don't need to tell me if you'd rather not."

Vivienne put down her cup and regarded it gloomily. "He asked me to marry him," she said. "I told him about you and Jethro, and he asked had I ever thought of marriage? I said, not lately, and then he said, 'I would like you to think of it now.'"

Nicola sipped at her coffee, intrigued. "Is that all?"

"Well no, there was quite a bit more." Vivienne picked up her cup again. "In the end, I said yes. Pietro is very persuasive when he turns on that Italian charm, and I . . . at my age it may seem silly to you, but I guess I've been in love with him for some time."

"It doesn't seem in the least silly," Nicola assured her. "I'm not surprised. He's a very attractive man."

"Mm. Also a very old-fashioned one. We began talking about practicalities, then. Where we'd live, for starters. . . . He assumed I'd give up this place. I didn't mind that; I quite looked forward to making a new home with him. But he also assumed that I'd give up my job."

"Oh." Nicola replaced her cup in its saucer.

"Yes, oh." Vivienne looked grim. "I couldn't seem to get it through to him that my work is more to me than a way of earning a living while I wait for Prince Charming to come and sweep me off my feet. He kept saying he had plenty of money for us both, that he'd make me a generous allowance and never question what I spent it on, and if I needed more at any time I only had to ask. Apart from the fact that I love what I do and wouldn't want to stop, that prospect didn't appeal to me in the least. I've never been financially dependent on a man in my life, and it's a bit late to start now. I couldn't bear the thought of ever having to ask him for money."

"He was very annoyed about it, wasn't he?"

"Very. He seemed to feel it impinged on his manhood. I know it's a cultural thing, and a generational one, too, I suppose. A lot of my contemporaries went into marriage with just that idea, the man being the breadwinner and the woman the housekeeper. And when there are children, of course it has to be that way . . . at least, it usually is unless they both work really hard at doing it differently. I've never thought of myself as a radical women's libber, but I suppose I've just gone ahead and done liberated things anyway."

"*Have* you ever thought of marriage before?" Nicola asked.

"Oh, yes. The first time . . . he died."

Nicola made a small sound of sympathy, and Vivienne said, "It's all right, it was twenty years ago and it hardly hurts anymore. I was at university, and I threw myself into my studies to get over the grief. I graduated with honours. Then I went to England and Europe for a while, taking various jobs, keeping my mind off things, and in time the worst passed. That was when I first worked in a publishing house and found that I loved it. And I began going out with men again. Maybe I'd idealised that first romance, but I could never feel for anyone else what I did for him. So, when proposals did come my way, I turned them down. And eventually I came to think that I wasn't cut out for marriage. I like being able to please myself about where I go and what I do, and what time I come home or when I leave a party. I like being able to buy things that I fancy without consulting someone else's taste—or his pocket —and being able to choose my own friends and go out with whoever I want to. I suppose it's a selfish life, but I was contented until . . ."

"Until Pietro came along," Nicola suggested.

Vivienne shrugged and smiled. "Yes. I told myself it was a last fling before middle age overtakes me, that I'd treat it lightly and take it as it came. Pietro's manner fooled me at first. You know how he is with women . . . all that flirtation, the way he looks at you as though you're the only woman in the room, the compliments flowing like wine. It's a heady mixture, but I told myself he didn't mean half of it, that he was just amusing himself. By the time I began to suspect he might be serious, I was at least half hoping that he was."

Nicola smiled. "So you wanted him to propose?"

"I must have been starry-eyed. It never occurred to me that he wouldn't want me to go on working. He used to tease me about my independence and call me a career woman, but I didn't realise he resented it so much."

"Don't you think that may be too strong a word? Once he adjusts to the idea he may come round."

Vivienne shook her head. "I doubt it. He doesn't even begin to understand why I won't give up my work. He's making it some kind of test of my feelings. If I won't do what he wants, it means that I'm not willing to accept all that marriage entails. He said if he'd wanted a mistress he could have asked one of several women." She smiled faintly. "I believe it, too. He wants a wife, someone who will really share his life and be 'the heart of his home.' I can't help feeling . . . proud that he asked me. Only I don't think I can be the kind of wife he really wants. All that he can see, of course, is that I don't love him enough to conform to his ideas."

"How much do you love him?"

Vivienne said slowly, "One part of me is very tempted to give in, but I know that if I did it wouldn't work. I'd miss my job, and probably feel resentful that he'd more or less forced me into giving it up. If I were younger it might be different. But I'm too old to start a family now, and looking after Pietro and his home and being his hostess wouldn't be enough to keep me occupied . . . and satisfied."

"Did you tell him that?"

Vivienne sighed. "I did try, but he was being terribly Latin and masterful and offended, and I don't think it really penetrated."

"Perhaps when he's had a chance to think it over . . ."

"I don't know. Maybe," Vivienne said doubtfully, and picked up the cups, taking them to the sink. "Anyway, don't let my troubles put a blight on your life. Have you and Jethro fixed a wedding date yet?"

"More or less." Nicola picked up the tea towel and wiped the cups as Vivienne rinsed them out and placed them on the draining board. "Three weeks from now, if my mother can get organised in time. We don't want a big wedding."

"Well, you don't mess about, do you? Or has Jethro bulldozed you?"

"Do you think I'd let him?"

Vivienne smiled. "I think you might . . . if you wanted to be bulldozed. Did you?"

Nicola shook her head, laughing. "No comment. Anyway, I'm going to bed. I hope you and Pietro work it out, Vivienne." She hung up the tea towel and turned to give the other woman an impulsive hug. "You deserve to be happy. Good-night."

There was a staff party on New Year's Eve, and Jethro took the opportunity to make a formal announcement of the engagement. After the party he took Nicola and Vivienne home, and as they sat in the lounge having coffee, Vivienne said, "Jethro, you're not going to take away my assistant, are you? I hope *you* don't have mediaeval ideas about working wives."

Jethro smiled. "Nicola can please herself. She needn't work if she doesn't want to. But perhaps she'd prefer to, at least until we start a family."

"I'll stay," Nicola assured her. "For a while, anyway. But as Jethro says . . ."

"Once you start a family, I know."

Jethro said curiously, "Who has mediaeval ideas about working wives?"

Vivienne looked away. "Oh, some men," she said vaguely.

Jethro gave her a penetrating glance and changed the subject. Vivienne excused herself soon afterward, saying she would have to get up early because she had been invited to go yachting with some friends.

Jethro, moving over to the sofa to join Nicola, said, "That was tactful of her." His arm slid about her shoulders.

"She *is* going out early," Nicola said.

"What about you? Coming with me to see my mother and Hank?"

"Yes, I'd like that. Have you told them. . . . ?"

"No. I'd like to tell them in person. We could stay overnight." He looked at her questioningly, correctly interpreted her uncertainty, and added, "There are two spare rooms."

"Well, if you're sure your mother won't mind. . . ."

"She'll be delighted. We won't need to leave at the crack of dawn if we're staying."

"Will they be able to come to the wedding?"

"I think so." His hand was absently stroking her arm. "What's bugging Vivienne?" he asked idly. "Do you know?"

"Mmm, but . . . I don't think she'd want me to tell everyone."

"I'm not 'everyone.' I'm your husband-to-be. . . . Is it that Italian bloke?"

Nicola stirred, making a slight movement away. He exerted a faint pressure, bringing her head to rest against his shoulder. His lips lightly touched her temple, then her cheek, and made a foray to the warm, hollowed skin below her ear. "She's old enough to know better," he murmured.

"Better than what?"

His mouth moved to her cheek. "Than to let that Latin charm sweep her off her feet." His hand turned her to face him, his mouth sliding to hers.

Nicola grasped his wrist and removed his hand, staring at him with slight hostility. "She hasn't, actually. Far from it. Don't you like Pietro?"

Jethro shrugged. "He's all right, I suppose. I can't help noticing the effect he has on women, though. I would have thought they'd know enough to add a large cup of salt to practically everything he says to them."

"They do add a pinch," she said coolly, "but at least what he says is a very pleasant change. Too many men in this country—and mine—wouldn't be caught dead paying a woman a compliment."

"Wouldn't you rather be given an occasional sincere compliment than be deluged with meaningless flattery?"

"Pietro isn't insincere," she argued. "He likes and admires women, and he's frank about telling them so. That's why women like him. You're not jealous, are you?"

"Of course I'm not jealous!" he said sharply.

"Then why don't you like him?"

"I already told you," he answered impatiently, "I don't dislike the man. I don't particularly want to talk about him, though. How did we get into this?"

"I don't know. You started it."

"Then I'll finish it." He reached for her with determination and pulled her into his arms. She returned his kiss, allowing him to part her lips and lay his hand on her breast as her head was pushed against the high back of the sofa. But when he began to slide her zipper down and made to lift her legs across his knees, she stopped him.

Jethro brought his hand back to her breast, stroking it, and murmured, "Can we go to your room?"

She shook her head and moved out of his embrace. "No," she said. "I'm sorry, but . . . not tonight, not here."

"Are you going to make me wait until we're married?" he asked, standing up.

"Is it too much to ask?" she challenged him, staring into his face.

He smiled wryly. "No. If that's what you want."

She didn't answer, and he smiled again, and bent and kissed her fiercely on the mouth. "See me out," he said. "I'll phone in the morning when I'm ready to leave."

She struggled awake to find the daylight filtering through the blinds and the telephone ringing insistently in the hall.

She stumbled out and lifted the receiver. Jethro's voice said, "Nicola? Are you awake?"

"No," she groaned.

He laughed. "Sorry. It never occurred to me you'd still be in bed."

"You, I suppose," she said bitterly, "have been up for hours."

"Hours," he agreed.

"What's the time?"

"Nearly ten," he told her.

"I don't believe it."

"Haven't you got a clock there?"

She peered at the watch still on her wrist. It had stopped. "I believe you," she mumbled.

"You're all right, aren't you?" he enquired suddenly.

"Yes," she said, warmed by the concern in his voice. "I was sleeping the sleep of the just, that's all."

"Of the virtuous, anyway," he said rather dryly. "When will you be ready to go?"

"Give me half an hour," she said, and then, "I could make us a picnic lunch if you give me a little longer."

"Thank you, darling, I'd like that."

She made a salad to go with slices of cold roast and salami, accompanied by a loaf of French bread from the freezer, with cheese and biscuits to follow. He had brought a bottle of Barossa Pearl, and when they stopped on a hill overlooking the sea and spread out the picnic it looked as appetising as a food and wine advertisement.

After they had eaten, he half lay on the grass, while Nicola sat a few feet away leaning against the bole of an old cabbage tree.

"You'll be the perfect wife," he said lazily, slanting her a teasing glance. "You can even cook."

Nicola laughed. "You can't call cold meat and salad cooking, exactly."

"It was delicious, anyway."

"You're easily pleased."

"A desirable trait in a husband, I should have thought."

It might be, but she didn't seriously think he was easily pleased. She knew that at work he demanded high standards, and there was evidence that the same went for his private life, too. She regarded him thoughtfully, and he leaned over, took her wrist, and gently tugged her down beside him, her head against his chest. She watched a white cloud slowly drift up from the horizon and disintegrate into small cottony shreds. The water shimmered in the sunlight, silver sparkles flashing on its restlessly moving surface. Jethro's chest rose and fell evenly beneath her cheek, and she lifted her head suddenly to look down at him.

His eyes questioned hers, and she said, "I thought you'd gone to sleep."

He smiled. "No. That would be a waste."

"Of what?"

"Opportunity," he answered and turned, so that she found herself lying on her back while he held her in his arms, his mouth coming down on hers in a long, exploring, satisfying kiss.

When he stopped kissing her, he looked down at her with an oddly speculative expression, and she said huskily, "Shouldn't we be getting on?"

He took one arm from under her, and looked at his watch. "I suppose so." He kissed her again, swiftly, and then got up, pulling her to her feet. "Come on, then. Stop this dilly-dallying, woman, and get a move on."

Chapter Nine

Jethro's mother received the news of the engagement with enthusiasm, and Hank shook Jethro's hand heartily and kissed Nicola's cheek as he congratulated them. Mrs. Porter gave Jethro a penetrating stare when he informed them that the wedding was to be in three weeks' time, and Jethro laughed and said, "No special reason for haste, Mother, except that we don't want to wait."

His mother gave him a reproving look and turned to Nicola. "Are you quite happy about that, my dear? Most girls would want a little more time to prepare."

"I don't mind," Nicola assured her. "But I'd like the wedding to be in New Zealand. Can you and Hank manage to come?"

"Wouldn't miss it for the world, would we?" Hank said. "Don't you worry, we'll be there."

The weekend passed pleasantly, and Nicola was glad

of the opportunity to get to know Jethro's mother and stepfather a little better. On Sunday she walked to church with Mrs. Porter, and on the way home said, "I really don't know a lot about Jethro's background . . . his childhood. He doesn't talk about it."

Mrs. Porter was silent for a while. Then she said slowly, "I suppose it wasn't very happy for him. Things were . . . difficult between my husband and myself for most of our married life. In the end, after Jethro grew up, I left him."

"I'm sorry," Nicola said. "I didn't mean to rake up painful memories."

"Oh, it's all right. Perhaps I should tell you a little about it, because Jethro won't, and it may help you if he's not always . . . easy to understand."

Nicola smiled faintly. "I've found that already."

"His father had a very violent temper. And an extremely jealous nature. The two combined were explosive, to say the least. He was even, in an odd sort of way, jealous of Jethro. I found that very hard. I realised that the rage and the jealousy about other men—ridiculous jealousy, I might add, because I never looked at anyone else after my marriage—were signs of insecurity. I tried to combat it by lavishing all my attention on my husband, pandering to him, as Jethro was to call it later. But I couldn't ignore my baby's needs, and there were times when his father had to take second place."

Privately, Nicola thought that Jethro's father sounded a very immature individual, but she waited for the other woman to continue her story.

"As Jethro grew older and more independent I tried to make it up to my husband, but I never dared have another baby. It would have been rather nice . . ." she said wistfully. "Perhaps a little girl . . . and my husband might even have liked a girl better . . . but I don't think I could have coped. Jethro was a rather withdrawn little boy, although he always did very well at school. But it wasn't until he left home and was away from his father's influence that he came out of his shell, and eventually he turned into the successful, apparently self-confident person that he is now. I still feel guilty about his upbringing, though. In some ways I feel he was deprived."

"He doesn't show signs of it," Nicola said. "I'd say he seems fairly well adjusted."

"Do you think so? Sometimes . . ." Her voice trailed off as they began to climb the slight slope to the house.

"Yes?" Nicola prompted.

"Well, I sometimes wondered if his emotions had been . . . crippled, in some way. He's been a long time deciding to get married. I was afraid he'd never fall in love . . . that perhaps he wouldn't allow himself to."

"There was Justine," Nicola reminded her.

"Yes." Mrs. Porter frowned slightly. "I'm not sure that he was in love with her. She always seemed such a cold person, somehow. I was afraid that Jethro might have decided to marry her merely because she was suitable and available, rather than from any deep feeling. I'm much happier about you, my dear. I think you'll be good for him, and I'm sure he knows it, too. But don't," she added as they climbed the steps to the verandah and she opened the front door, "allow him to throw his weight around too much. My mistake was in letting my husband bully me, until he believed it was his right. When I began to think I should stick up for myself, it was too late for both of us. I'd lost the ability, and he had become accustomed to using me as a doormat. I love my son dearly, and he has quite different methods, but I've noticed as he's grown up that, in his own quiet fashion, Jethro is really remarkably like his father in many ways."

She stopped abruptly in the doorway, so that Nicola very nearly cannoned into her. Then she moved inside, saying rather too brightly, "Good morning, Jethro. We've been to church."

Jethro's cool reply was a fraction delayed, and Nicola glanced at his mother, realising that he must have overheard. Before either of the women could say anything, though, he was saying, "I've made coffee. Anyone want bacon and eggs?"

"We'll have to go to this," Jethro said a few days later, tossing a gilt-edged invitation onto Nicola's desk. "It's just before the wedding, I'm afraid, but I can't not be there, and you'd better come, too."

It was an invitation to a literary prize-giving. One of the books short-listed for the prize was Jessica Seymour's *Prisoners in Petticoats*.

"I'd like to go," Nicola said. "Especially if Jess is a likely winner."

"She has an outside chance," Jethro conceded, "but there's some stiff competition. Two of the contenders are well-known, established writers."

The occasion was a glittering one. Vivienne, as Jess's editor, had also been invited. She looked lovely in a lavender-grey dress with a small spray of violets at her throat, and Nicola had opted for champagne silk in a simple style with a softly draped neckline that dipped low in front. Jethro, calling for them, said, "You both look fantastic. I'm proud to escort such beauty."

Vivienne said, "Good gracious, such extravagance from you, Jethro! Have you been coaching him, Nicola, in how to compliment a woman?"

"I don't need coaching," Jethro growled. "Pietro Benotti isn't the only man around who appreciates a beautiful woman or recognises the fact that she's made a special effort."

Vivienne almost visibly flinched, and Nicola cast Jethro a look of such indignation that he blinked.

"What did I say?" he murmured as, after ensconcing Vivienne in the back seat, he opened the front passenger door for Nicola.

"Never mind," Nicola muttered. There wasn't time to explain, and anyway, Vivienne hadn't given her permission to pass on the story of her personal troubles to Jethro or anyone else.

Nicola was glad to meet Jess and Gareth again. She was less thrilled when she caught a glimpse of Justine Canham among the hundred or so guests, and wondered how she had come by her invitation. She seemed to be with a rather tubby, balding man who had melting brown eyes and a neatly trimmed, greying beard. He looked distinguished but was hardly a glamorous foil for Justine's dark beauty.

When the first prizewinner was announced, he bounded up onto the stage to receive a cheque and certificate and to make a short, quite brilliant speech. Nicola had heard of him but had never seen his face before. His winning was obviously no surprise to anyone.

Jess, to her great pleasure, won second place. Accepting their congratulations, she said, "I must thank you, Jethro, and Vivienne, for accepting the book and publishing it. It's marvellous to know that some people think it's this good."

"The prize should boost sales too," Jethro told her. "How would you like to do a small publicity tour?"

Jess grimaced. "Not my scene. I'd rather be writing."

Jethro laughed. "So would most writers. But such things help to sell books."

"I think my work should sell on its own merit, not

because I happen to be around to autograph a few copies."

"Very noble," Jethro scoffed. "But they won't buy it if they've never heard of it. . . ."

Nicola excused herself to slip away to the ladies' room. It was quite opulent, with gilt-framed mirrors and imitation Louis Quinze chairs, and a thick red carpet on the floor. As she sat on one of the chairs and refreshed her lipstick, the door swung open and Justine swept into the room.

Nicola said cautiously, "Hello."

"Oh." Justine seemed disconcerted. "Hello. Nicola, isn't it? You're here with Jethro, of course."

"Yes," Nicola said. "And you're with the grand-prize winner, aren't you? You must be very proud."

With a slight look of surprise, Justine said, "Yes—yes, I am, of course." She came forward to the mirror and studied her reflection critically, touching her hair and smoothing her eyebrows.

"Is he a relative?" Nicola asked politely.

Justine cast her an amused glance. "Not yet. I'm going to marry him, as a matter of fact."

"Marry him?"

Her startled tone brought Justine round to face her. "Why not?"

Embarrassed, Nicola said hastily, "I'm sorry. It's just . . . at first sight I'd have thought . . ."

"That he's not my type?" Justine suggested. "Oh, I know, he's not as handsome as Jethro. But he's extremely successful at what he does, and he has a simply wonderful mind. The fact that he's . . . plain is an asset in my book."

Nicola blinked.

Justine said, "Look, I was hard on you last time we . . . met. I'm not good at apologising, but for what it's worth, I didn't much like what I saw myself doing that night." She looked down at her nails, studying them with apparent care. "I'm not surprised that Jethro threw me over. I always knew he disliked any display of emotion . . . with the possible exception of sexual passion, which doesn't turn many men off." She gave Nicola a wry look. "Our . . . courtship. . . . was a very coldblooded affair in other ways. He'd decided he needed a wife, and I had got to the stage where my career wasn't enough for me. He liked me because I seemed to be in charge of my own destiny, full of admirable qualities like independence and self-control. He once told me that he can't bear 'clinging, helpless women.' Well, I tried to be all that he wanted. Only I made the mistake of falling in love with the brute. And when I'm in love, I get . . . jealous. That's a very destructive emotion. I intend to steer clear of it in future."

"What about . . . ?"

"Gerry?" She laughed indulgently. "He could have all the women he wanted if he didn't have such a strong conviction that he's ugly. As it is, he adores me, and I'm extremely fond of him. We're right for each other. Jethro would have made me miserable. What about you and him? Are you going together?"

"We're engaged."

Justine smiled. "Engaged? Well, good luck to you. You'll need it." She raised her eyes and sighed. "And I didn't mean that to sound catty."

"I know you didn't." Nicola put away her lipstick and stood up, holding out her hand. "And I hope you'll be very happy."

"You too." Justine's clasp was firm, but her eyes held a doubt.

Nicola smiled. "Thank you." She withdrew her

hand, and for a moment they looked at each other with friendly acceptance, before Nicola went out and walked through the chattering crowd to Jethro's side.

"Okay?" he asked her as he drew her into the circle of his arm.

"Yes," she answered. "Have you seen Justine to-night?"

"Justine?" His face went cold.

"You must have noticed," she said, "that she's with the guest of honour."

Reluctantly he admitted, "Yes."

"Well, aren't you going to congratulate him?"

"He's surrounded by well-wishers."

"There'll be a chance sooner or later," Nicola said serenely. "And I think you should speak to Justine too."

"What the devil are you playing at?" he asked softly.

"Peacemaking, I suppose," she said, smiling up at him. "I think you were too hard on her, and if you can't bring yourself to apologise, you might at least be civilised enough to wish her well. She's going to marry that man."

"How do you know?"

"She just told me. And she also . . . almost . . . apologised for the way she behaved toward me. I think it was very handsome of her."

"*I* think it was the least she could do."

"And I think the least you can do is talk to her nicely for a few minutes."

"I don't know what you're up to. . . ."

"I'm not up to anything. It's a simple matter of decent, reasonable behaviour."

His brows rose, and he gave her an ironic bow. "Okay," he said. "But if she claws my eyes out, on your head be it."

Nicola laughed. "She won't."

Of course she didn't. The meeting was accomplished without any complications at all, and afterward, as he led her away, Jethro murmured in Nicola's ear, "Satisfied?"

"Thank you," she said sincerely. She didn't know exactly what had been accomplished by it, but she felt that in the few minutes Jethro and Justine had spent together without rancour, a faint shadow over her own future with Jethro had been dispelled.

The short flight across the Tasman was accomplished in beautiful, clear weather, and Nicola's family awaited them at the airport, eager to see Jethro for the first time. He stayed at a hotel for the three days prior to the wedding, and his mother and Hank joined him on the wedding eve. Vivienne flew over too, along with a married couple who were old friends of Jethro's.

When Nicola entered the church on her father's arm and saw Jethro waiting for her, looking grave and extremely handsome and very tall, he suddenly seemed a stranger. Then she saw him smile, and she smiled back with serene confidence.

After the ceremony they had a quiet celebration at her home and later in the day drove south to Rotorua, because Jethro had expressed a curiosity to see the place.

"It smells," Nicola warned him as they drew close to the small city several hours after leaving Auckland. Already sulphurous fumes could be seen rising occasionally from vents in the earth's crust near the roadside.

Jethro sniffed. "Mm—I suppose one gets used to it."

Their hotel had a spa pool supplied from a bore that tapped one of the hot streams and springs lying underground throughout the city. After unpacking, they went down and spent a pleasant, relaxing half hour in it, before entering the dining room for the evening meal.

They ate in leisurely fashion, and were lingering over coffee when a man leaving the room stopped behind Jethro's chair, exclaiming, "Nicola!"

Nicola looked up into Robin's eyes, her own startled and dismayed. "Robin!"

Jethro's head whipped round; he eyed the other man, then got to his feet. "Introduce me," he said to Nicola, his expression giving nothing away.

"Robin Lynch," she said automatically. "Robin, this is Jethro Vallance."

"I'm Nicola's husband," Jethro said suavely, holding out his hand.

"Husband!" Robin allowed his hand to be taken, his gaze on Nicola's face. "I didn't know you were getting married."

Slightly nettled as well as embarrassed, Nicola said shortly, "Well, I have. How's your wife?"

Robin looked discomfited. "Fine, fine, thanks," he said vaguely. "Well, it's been nice meeting you. . . ."

But Jethro said, "Why don't you join us in the bar for a drink? And your wife, of course."

"Oh, she isn't with me. I'm here for a conference, actually. Business, you know."

"Well, just you, then," Jethro insisted. "Come on, darling," he said, turning to Nicola. "You've finished your coffee, haven't you? Let's continue the conversation in more comfortable surroundings."

As far as she was concerned, Nicola wished the conversation had finished five minutes ago, or preferably had never even started, but she allowed Jethro to pull out her chair and take her elbow as they went to one of the cosy hotel bars. All the while Jethro questioned Robin about the conference, and when they reached the bar he placed her between them on a curved banquette before ordering drinks all round.

Jethro appeared to be perfectly at ease, and Robin soon lost his initial restraint and responded eagerly to every remark addressed to him, while Nicola quietly seethed, growing more and more acutely uncomfortable.

At length, with the men discussing the danger to the city's tourist attractions posed by the indiscriminate tapping of its natural energy resources, she could bear it no longer and got to her feet, saying, "If you'll excuse me, I think I'll go to our room. Good-night, Robin."

Jethro rose to let her pass him, but didn't attempt to accompany her, merely handing her one of the room keys and saying casually, "I'll be there shortly, darling."

Without glancing at him, she swept up the stairs, disdaining to take the lift, and when she reached the room, slammed the door and sank down on one of the beds. She couldn't believe what was happening. This was her wedding night, and her husband was downstairs chatting to her ex-fiancé while she sat alone in their room. It was farcical.

Angrily she dragged out her case and began to unpack the filmy apricot nightdress and matching wrap she had bought specially for this occasion. A long, hot shower, unnecessary though it was after the session in the spa earlier, made her feel slightly better, and she emerged from the bathroom to find that Jethro had returned and was standing by the window, his shirt unbuttoned, the bed beside him turned down.

His eyes ran over her in a lightning assessment, and he began to smile. "You look delectable," he said, coming toward her. "I've been waiting for you."

"I didn't hear you come in."

"I told you I wouldn't be long." He reached her and curved his arms loosely about her, looking at the low neckline of the nightgown and back again to her face.

"I'm surprised you could tear yourself away," she said tartly.

His brows rose, and he laughed a little. "It's supposed to be proper to give one's bride time to . . . prepare herself, isn't it? And I must say, you've made good use of the time I gave you."

He bent to kiss her, but her lips remained unresponsive. "What's the matter?" he asked, raising his head again to look into her eyes.

"You must have realised who Robin was?"

"If I hadn't, your reactions would have told me unmistakably."

"Why on earth did you ask him to have a drink with us?" she demanded.

He shrugged. "It seemed the civilised thing to do."

"Civilised!"

"Don't you think so?"

She stared at him. "Oh, yes," she agreed sarcastically. "Very."

"Would you rather I'd punched him in the nose?"

"Of course not. I'd rather have ignored him. Especially tonight."

His eyes gleamed. "Did it bother you, seeing him?"

"No. It bothered me that you seemed to find his company more compelling than mine."

Jethro laughed, then he kissed her again, with hungry insistence, and this time she forced herself to respond, telling herself it was stupid to let the incident upset her, and the last thing she wanted was a quarrel. He brought her closer to him, bending back her head against his encircling arm, and parted her lips with his tongue. After a while her response became genuine and passionate, and he lifted her in his arms and carried her the few steps to the bed. He made love to her with fierce passion that at last overwhelmed her, and her husky little moans of pleasure brought low, triumphant laughter from him before he stifled them with his lips as they both rode a wave of unbelievable ecstasy.

Their honeymoon was short but satisfying. She had seen Robin in the distance on the second day, and then he apparently left. Jethro never mentioned him again, and she certainly didn't want to. Robin was a closed chapter of her life. Another chapter with Jethro was just beginning. He was a demanding yet considerate lover, and she knew that he delighted in her increasingly uninhibited responses. In the daytime they explored the weird landscape of boiling mudpools, geysers that shot roaring from the holes in the ground, and steaming rocks covered with brilliant yellow sulphur and white lime deposits; or they drove to one of the lakes that lay in a basin of gentle hills covered in thick native bush, or picnicked by a stream teeming with trout and fed by a crystal-clear spring bubbling up from some subterranean river. Each night they conducted a different kind of exploration, finding the boundaries of their ability to please and take pleasure in each other. Nicola felt that a bond was being created between them that would strengthen their marriage for all the years to come.

It wasn't until their return to Sydney that the first cracks appeared in her happiness.

Chapter Ten

They found a lovely modern house overlooking the harbour, and Jethro said, "We should have a house-warming party. Some of my friends don't even know I'm married, and most of them couldn't come to the wedding."

"I'm not an experienced hostess," Nicola said. "I hope your friends don't mind if it's very informal."

"We'll get in a professional caterer," Jethro suggested. "I've always done that before, and it means that you can enjoy yourself with the guests and not get tired out beforehand."

Perusing the guest list, Nicola said, "I don't know if we can fit in all these people."

"It's still warm enough for some to sit out on the patio, even though they might not want to use the pool."

"Mmm. What about lights?"

"We could rig some more, but the old coach lantern

out there casts enough of a romantic glow. People will only be talking, or dancing, or . . . Not reading the newspaper, anyway." He grinned. "They won't need a lot of light."

The patio was a sheltered, paved area overhung by an old fig tree and some smaller shrubs and opening onto the swimming pool, which was one of the chief attractions of the house. In the last days of summer it was a pleasant, cool retreat where they sometimes ate their evening meal. On the night of the party people did spill over from the house to use it. Checking that everyone was happy and having a good time, Nicola wandered out there close to midnight, and as she passed by a trellis covered with ivy geranium, smelled smoke. There were not many people left on the patio, since the air was growing chilly, and nobody nearby seemed to have a cigarette.

Puzzled, she walked around the trellis, and saw a tall, shadowy figure with a glowing light in one hand. The man turned as she stopped, and said, "Ah, Nicola. Forgive me, you've caught me being unsociable."

"Pietro." She went toward him, wondering why he had come out there to smoke a solitary cigar. "I smelled the smoke, and wondered. . . . I didn't realise it was a cigar."

His teeth gleamed white in the darkness. "No, it is not some incendiary setting fire to your wonderful old trees. This is a beautiful spot, a place . . . for lovers."

His voice sounded deeply melancholy, his accent strong, and she suppressed a smile at the deliberate pathos of it.

She had invited him because she liked him, and with an ulterior motive. She hoped to give him and Vivienne a chance to reconcile their differences, and if they didn't . . . well, there were enough people for them to avoid each other's company if they so chose.

Apparently Pietro had so chosen. For the moment he was avoiding not only Vivienne but everyone at the party. Vivienne, on the other hand, appeared to have thrown off her recent mood of quiet withdrawal and seemed to be thoroughly enjoying herself. She had abandoned her usual pastel colours for a dramatic black sheath with deep silk fringing, and black stockings and high-heeled pumps that showed off her pretty legs. Jethro had raised his brows in surprise, and Nicola told her sincerely that she looked sensational. At least two of the other men at the party obviously thought so too, but Pietro hadn't gone near her after an initial chilly greeting, and Nicola had watched him glowering across the room for some time before her duties as hostess distracted her attention.

Jethro had not wanted Pietro at all, querying her decision to add his name to the guest list.

"We hardly know the man," he objected.

"I hardly know most of the people *you* want to invite," she retorted. "And I happen to like Pietro very much."

"Something's happened between him and Vivienne, hasn't it? Will she want him invited? I haven't seen them together lately."

"It's our party, not Vivienne's."

"I don't want her made uncomfortable."

"*I* want Pietro to be at the party."

"Why?"

"I told you, I like him!"

"Supposing I say that I *don't* want him?"

Suddenly flaring, Nicola had said, "You're being absolutely unreasonable. What on earth have you got against Pietro?"

"I don't have to give reasons. This is my home, and if I don't choose to invite him, I don't have to."

"Oh, so it's *your* home, is it?" Nicola said sarcastically. "And your party too, I suppose. I'm sorry. As your wife, I thought I might have some say. . . ."

Stiffly, Jethro said, "I didn't mean to imply that. . . ."

"Well, it sure sounded like it!"

"There's no need to lose your temper," he said quietly, his eyes narrowing as he surveyed her flushed cheeks and defiant gaze. "If it means that much to you, you'd better invite him."

Then he turned abruptly and left the room.

Later he had given every sign of having forgotten the small contretemps. Nicola, still smarting, had nevertheless followed his lead, deciding it was useless pursuing the subject once she had won her point. Every married couple had disagreements, and this one probably only hurt so much because it was the first.

Jethro had greeted Pietro when he arrived with the same courtesy he afforded to the other guests, and Nicola had given him an especially warm smile. She was aware, though, that he was not enjoying himself, and wondered whether she had, after all, done the wrong thing in inviting him. Now, finding him uncharacteristically alone in the darkness, she said frankly, "I'm sorry that you're not happy, Pietro."

He shrugged. "How do you know that?"

"It isn't like you to go off on your own at a party." Carefully, she added, "Vivienne has been unhappy too, lately."

He took a draw on the cigar. "She seems to have recovered, then," he said. "She is obviously enjoying herself very much tonight."

Nicola had her doubts about that, but if Vivienne was eager to give that impression, it didn't seem fair to suggest otherwise. Trying an oblique approach, she said, "I don't think that Vivienne is a shallow person."

Again he drew on his cigar before answering, gazing

down at the glowing tip. "She has confided in you," he said. It was not a question. "I don't think she is shallow, either, but her feelings for me didn't go very deep, did they?"

"I think they do."

"Do?" He raised his head sharply.

"Surely you don't imagine she could just stop caring in a matter of weeks. Have *you?*"

"Of course not. But appearances would suggest . . ."

"Appearances can be misleading. For instance, if I didn't know better, I would say you didn't give a hoot for Vivienne."

"That's not true!"

"I know. But you've been doing your best to give that impression."

"It was she who turned down my proposal."

"Because you wanted her to give up working."

He made an impatient gesture. "Is that so unreasonable? There is no need—"

"Yes, there *is!* Vivienne needs it. Oh, I don't suppose it's any use arguing about it—you and Vivienne must have thrashed it out pretty thoroughly—but I wish you would try and see her point of view."

"I have tried. She called me mediaeval, and I suppose she's right. I have very old-fashioned views on some things. I have never particularly liked career women."

"Vivienne's a career woman, and you do like her."

"Yes. I love her, but . . ."

"But not enough to let her be herself. You want to change her into someone else . . . a different kind of person from the one you fell in love with."

"That's nonsense! Simply giving up her job . . ."

". . . would be giving up a large part of her life.

You're trying to turn her into the kind of wife you think you want . . . perhaps make her over into the image of your first wife . . . but she isn't like anyone else. She's herself . . . a career woman, among other things. If you can't accept her as she is, then you don't deserve her."

He raised a hand to his hair, and turned abruptly, taking several strides away from her, and smoking furiously for a while. At last he said, "You're very blunt, Nicola."

"I'm fond of Vivienne, and I like you too, Pietro."

"So you're playing matchmaker, eh?"

"I know it's none of my business . . ."

"It's all right. You're concerned about your friend. I'm flattered that you think, in spite of my shortcomings, I might make her a good husband. But first you want to reform me, no?"

"If you could just be a little more tolerant . . ."

"Yes, it is not one of my virtues." He paused, and came back to stand close to her. The cigar had burned down, and he dropped it in the grass and ground it out with his shoe. "I will tell you something," he said. "You mentioned my first wife. . . ."

"I'm sorry, I shouldn't have . . ."

He raised a hand. "No, no, it's all right. You've made me think . . . and I begin to see things I've been blind to in the past. I loved my wife very much; she gave me two sons, and she was a beautiful woman, and always her first care was to please me." He paused, looking at the ground. "You know Claire, of course," he said. "My step-daughter."

"Yes." The Carvers had been invited that night but had not been able to come because of a previous engagement.

"I never knew of her existence until after my wife

died," Pietro said. "It was a terrible shock to me, not only that Gail could have kept such a secret through all the years of our marriage, but that so sweet and loving a person could have been so cruel as to abandon her child, leaving her in a convent orphanage to be brought up by the nuns."

Nicola failed to suppress a small sound of horror, and Pietro said, "Yes, it seems unbelievable to me, too. For a time I was very angry, very . . . bewildered. And she was no longer here to be confronted with my feelings, my questions. I could only guess that she had been afraid of my reaction to the news that she had a child already—she had not been married before—and that she kept putting it off until it was too late. She hated unpleasantness, and she was not strong-willed. If I lost my temper she would cry. I had to remember always to be patient with her."

She sounded very different, Nicola thought, from Vivienne who, although even-tempered and very feminine, was independent and strong-minded and unlikely to burst into tears when confronted with an angry male.

Pietro said slowly, "Poor Gail tried very hard to be the kind of wife I wanted . . . the kind of person she imagined I thought she should be. And it led to her doing something monstrous . . . because she was so afraid of displeasing me, of not living up to my . . . expectations. I must take some of the blame for that. I was selfish and egotistical. And I've been doing the same sort of thing with Vivienne. You're right, Nicola. I was trying to force her into being something she could never be, making the same mistake all over again. What a terrible person I am! I'm surprised that you can bring yourself to like me at all."

"I do like you. A lot," Nicola said, impulsively giving him a hug. "And I'm sure Vivienne does too, and if you tell her that you'll try to understand, and ask for another chance, I'll be very surprised if she turns down the offer."

His arm came round her shoulders, and he looked down at her face. "Thank you. But I'm afraid I angered her very much the last time we spoke."

"Perhaps it won't hurt you to eat a little humble pie," Nicola suggested.

"Not my favourite dish." He grimaced. "You women, you like your little bit of revenge, don't you?"

"I'm sure revenge isn't at all what Vivienne wants."

"No," he said soberly. "She has a generous nature. And you, too. Jethro is a lucky man. Thank you again, Nicola." He lifted her chin with his finger and dropped a light kiss on her lips, then brought both his arms around her in an exuberant hug. "Wish me luck," he said.

"Yes, of course." She put her arms about his neck and kissed his cheek before stepping back. "She might let you take her home."

"I doubt it." He began walking back to the patio with his arm companionably about her waist. "But I will certainly see her again soon, and make her listen to me."

There was no one on the patio now. Nicola picked up a few empty glasses and an ashtray and took them into the kitchen, where the caterers were washing up, while Pietro went back to the living room. A few minutes later, as she entered the crowded room, she saw him purposefully make his way to Vivienne's side, in the most courteous way possible shouldering aside her two admirers and escorting her, with a masterful hand on her waist, to a more private corner, where he bent close to her and spoke rapidly, the movements of his hands emphasising the urgency of his speech.

Jethro said in her ear, "Some of the guests have left. They couldn't find you to say good-bye."

"Oh, I'm sorry!" She turned to him. "I've been . . ."

"Never mind. Jess and Gareth are going now. Come and see them off."

From then on the party thinned. Vivienne went home in a taxi, but Pietro whispered to Nicola as he left shortly afterward, "I'm to see her tomorrow, so it's not hopeless."

As she closed the door behind him, smiling slightly, Jethro said, "Secrets?"

"Sort of."

Jethro's brows went up, but someone else came into the hall, ready to say goodnight, and the moment was lost.

With everyone gone, Nicola had begun emptying ashtrays into a paper bag when Jethro came into the room and said, "Why not leave that until the morning?"

"The room will smell. It won't take long. You go to bed, if you like."

"I've a better idea," he said, strolling over and taking the bag from her hand as she put down the last ashtray. He went through to the kitchen and quickly disposed of the bag before returning to her, catching her by the waist as she made to straighten the cushions on the sofa.

"Come on," he said, "let's both go to bed."

Nicola smiled listlessly. In spite of having professionals provide the food, organising their first party had been an exhausting, if enjoyable, task. "I'm rather tired," she confessed.

For an answer he caught her up in his arms, swinging her off her feet. "You don't even have to walk."

He put her down on the bed and undressed her, pulling the covers up over her nakedness before removing his own clothes. As he slid into the bed beside her, she said apologetically, "I really am tired, Jethro."

"If you're not too tired for tidying up," he said, "you're not too tired for this."

As his lips closed over hers, she tried to avoid the kiss, indignant that he chose to ignore her feelings, but he caught at her hair, imprisoning her under his invading mouth. She was too tired to fight him, too, and at last under his increasingly passionate caresses a faint warm stirring of response seeped through her, and she shivered and almost reluctantly pressed closer to him, still a little resentful and slightly shocked at the selfishness of his behaviour. Her body felt limp and boneless, and her head swam with fatigue, but her breathing quickened as his hands explored her with an intimacy that made her shudder again with sluggish pleasure, and he didn't seem to notice that she was giving him little more than quiescent acceptance.

When at last he left her, Nicola touched her tongue to bruised lips and turned away. He went very still, and after a few moments got up and went into the bathroom. She lay looking at the darkness, dry-eyed but weeping inside. Perhaps he had drunk a little too much; that might have made him less considerate than usual.

He came back and got into the bed, then leaned over and stroked her hair back from her cold cheek and said, "I'm sorry."

The apology helped, although she doubted he had more than an inkling of what he had just done to her. Her lids drooped; she felt dizzy with fatigue. In a few minutes she had fallen asleep.

Vivienne said nothing about Pietro on Monday, but several times in the following weeks Nicola caught her gazing into space in a thoughtful way.

On the surface, her own marriage was running smoothly. There had been no repetition of the events that had followed the party . . . but then, she reminded herself uneasily, she had never again needed to plead tiredness. She still found their lovemaking exquisitely satisfying, and in that department she had no complaints. But it seemed to her that they were in many respects growing further apart. When they went out as a twosome they seemed to recapture some of the intimacy they had once shared, and Nicola came to cherish these rare occasions. But if they were at a party, she would often turn from a conversation with someone to find that Jethro had left her side, and it might be an hour or more before he rejoined her. At home they talked lightly of inconsequential topics, but if she tried to turn the conversation to their own relationship he would change the subject. They never quarrelled, for if she showed any sign of irritability Jethro became coldly poker-faced and simply withdrew until she regained her temper and remembered how he hated scenes. Later he would come back and make some coolly courteous remark and restore the status quo. And Nicola, ashamed of herself for nearly losing control over some trivial issue, would respond in kind, helping to smooth over the awkward moment.

At last Vivienne came to work one day wearing a diamond solitaire ring on the third finger of her left hand, and stopped by Nicola's desk to say, "I believe I have you to thank for this."

"Pietro?" Nicola asked, jumping to her feet.

"Of course, Pietro," Vivienne answered. "He finally persuaded me that he, at least, is not too old a leopard to have changed his spots."

"But it's been weeks!" Nicola exclaimed. "I didn't think anything was happening."

"Oh, it's happened. I must admit, I was suspicious of his about-face at first. I was afraid that he was just talking, and that once we were married he'd change his mind again. But do you know he hasn't made one snide remark about career women since the night of your party? He told me that you and he had a heart-to-heart talk, and that started him thinking."

Jethro came in the door, a red folder in one hand. "You and who?" he asked Nicola.

Vivienne turned to him, flourishing her ring. "Pietro," she said.

"Pietro." The closed look came down over his face, and Nicola inwardly sighed. Surely he wasn't going to let his absurd prejudice against Pietro blight Vivienne's happy day.

"He and Vivienne are getting married," she said, trying to signal him with her eyes to look pleased, even if he didn't feel it. "Isn't it marvellous?"

Strangely, he looked at her first, then at Vivienne. He took the hand with the ring on it and studied it, then looked up into Vivienne's face and slowly smiled. "Marvellous," he agreed, and bent to kiss her cheek. "I wish you every happiness, Viv. Are you going to leave us?"

Vehemently, Vivienne shook her head. "Not at all. I'll be right here."

"He doesn't mind? I thought he was something of a traditionalist."

"Not since talking to your wife." Vivienne grinned.

Nicola studied her nails with a smug smile. "The best matchmaker in the business," she said, and laughed.

"All right, you can be pleased with yourself," Vivienne conceded. "Meantime, I'd better start some work, seeing the boss is here."

She crossed to her desk, and Jethro, turning to Nicola, said, "You are, aren't you?"

"I am what?"

"Pleased with yourself."

She nodded, unable to stop smiling. "I like seeing my friends happy, and I think they're right for each other."

He gave her a rather odd look, and turned to put the folder on Vivienne's desk.

Over coffee in the living room after dinner that evening, he brought up the subject again. "Is that what you and Pietro were having that long tête-à-tête about on the night of our housewarming? His relationship with Vivienne?"

"Yes." Then, staring at him, she asked, "How did you know we had a long tête-à-tête?"

Jethro stared into his coffee cup. "I saw you."

"You saw us?"

"You'd been missing for ages," he said. "I went looking for you." He put down his cup on the side table suddenly and stood up, walking away from her to the other side of the room. "I did wonder," he said, "what sort of discussion it was . . . that included him kissing you."

He had turned to face her now, and she still stared, the coffee cup in her hand forgotten. "Kissing me?" she repeated.

"He did kiss you, didn't he?"

"Well, yes . . . in a friendly sort of way."

"It looked very friendly from where I was standing."

"Jethro!" she said, stunned. "Are you . . . accusing me of something?"

"*No!*" he said vehemently. One of his hands left his pocket and pushed violently into his hair. "No," he said, "of course not. Forget it. I shouldn't have mentioned it."

"Why not, if it bothers you?" she demanded. "And it obviously does!"

"Leave it. It doesn't matter."

He made to go out of the room, and she said sharply, "Jethro, wait!" She put her cup down and ran to put her hand on his arm. "You always walk away," she said. "Stop walking away from me."

"It's the only alternative," he said. "Let me go, Nicola." He shook off her hand and kept walking.

She darted in front of him, holding on to both his arms. "Alternative to what?" she demanded.

He grasped her shoulders and put her aside quite roughly. "I said, *leave* it!" His face was pale and set, and without glancing at her again he went on his way to his study.

As she watched the door shut behind him, Nicola suddenly exploded into pure rage. She marched across the hall, flung open the door and stormed into the room. "Don't you dare shut a door in my face!" she cried. "I know you don't like scenes, but this time you'll just have to lump it! If you won't talk to me, you're going to have to put up with being yelled at by me. Because I'm tired of bottling up my anger and being civilised and genteel and never showing my feelings!"

A frown appeared between his brows as he stood watching her, but she refused to be intimidated. "You'd like me to be 'serene' and 'restful' and 'dignified,'" she went on. "Well, at the moment I don't feel like that! I'm angry, and I'm hurt and frustrated, and I'm not going to dam it all up because you think it's unwomanly or unladylike or whatever. I can't live my life according to some totally unrealistic picture of me that you've got fixed in your mind. I'm sick of trying to live up to some image of an ideal woman you hoped you'd married. I'm human and I'm real and I have emotions, and I can't always control them. I told Pietro he was trying to make Vivienne into someone else. Well, you're doing the same thing to me!"

"You don't understand." He was standing by the desk holding himself rigid. "We'll talk later, when you've calmed down—"

Nicola clenched her teeth. "We will not! We'll talk *now!* I have no intention of calming down. I love you, like it or not . . ." She saw something flare in his eyes as his head jerked up, but she went on. ". . . and you can't take my love and try to stifle every other emotion that I have. . . . It doesn't work that way. It's all or nothing."

He cast her a look of such fierce hunger that she was stopped in her tracks. "Then I'll take all," he said quietly.

For a moment she couldn't even speak. Some of her anger had been dissipated. Then, taking the bull by the horns, she said, "Just what did you think when you saw Pietro kissing me?"

His mouth hardened, and she saw the tension in his jaw. "I didn't think anything," he said doggedly.

"You were jealous!"

"No!" He suddenly brought his fist down with a thud on the desk. "Nicola, stop this!"

"Why didn't you mention it to me?" she demanded ruthlessly. "Why didn't you come over to us at the time and ask us what was going on?"

He turned on her so suddenly that she recoiled. "Because I won't *do* that to you!" he said forcefully. "I won't start subjecting you to an inquisition every time my imagination runs riot. I won't make our marriage the kind of battlefield that my parents' marriage became. *I don't want to be like that.*"

"He hugged me," she said. "Out of gratitude, mainly. And sheer Italian emotionalism. He kissed me, very lightly, a peck. And I kissed his cheek. That's what happened, Jethro. You believe me, don't you?"

"Of course I believe you! I've always known it was something like that . . . in my sane moments."

She went over to him, taking his clenched fist in her hands, straightening out the fingers until she could intertwine them with her own. "You're afraid of being like your father, aren't you?" she asked him.

"I'm more like him than I ever knew. When I heard my mother say so, I rejected it utterly. Now . . . I realise you were right when you said I should apologise to Justine. They say one sees one's own faults most clearly in someone else. If I'd ever loved her as I love you we'd have torn each other apart. When we met Robin on our honeymoon I had an almost overwhelming urge to thump him on the spot for what he did to you . . . and for what he'd been to you."

"But . . . you invited him to join us for drinks!"

"I was trying to match your . . . sophistication and generosity. I remembered your attitude to Justine. I managed to weather meeting Robin without showing how I felt. Then, when I saw you and Pietro . . . I quite simply wanted to kill him. That's when I realised the danger to our marriage. If I felt like that over what my head kept telling me was a perfectly harmless little episode, I could wreck our happiness if I ever allowed myself to start putting you through any kind of third degree about it."

"A simple question isn't a third degree," Nicola pointed out.

"I couldn't trust myself to stop at a simple question. I don't think you realise how much I love you, and how . . . afraid I am of losing you. I promised myself I wouldn't make you spend every waking moment with me; I wouldn't stick to you like glue at parties; I wouldn't try to smother you, or act as though I owned you; I'd behave like a rational human being and never put you in a cage of love and jealousy."

"I don't think you have any idea," Nicola said softly, "how much I love you!"

"I've never been sure you did. Looking back, I realise just how much like my father I really am. I'm as much of a selfish bully as he ever was, in my own way. I kept telling myself to give you the breathing space you asked for, but every time I saw you I wanted you so badly that I'd start putting the pressure on. I bullied you into marrying me, and it serves me right that because of that I've never been sure of you."

"I do love you," Nicola said. "I wouldn't have married you otherwise, and no amount of bullying would have made me do it. I love you terribly, but if you don't know that, it's because I was afraid to show it. I miss you when you leave me talking to other people at parties. I *want* you to be by my side. You're not my jailor, you're my husband. I chose to be yours, to have and to hold. You've got a right to know what I'm doing kissing another man, even if it is an innocent little peck. If I'd known you'd seen it I would have told you without hesitation. I've been feeling so left out lately, so . . . repressed, because you've been aloof and cold and . . . I thought you were trying to make me like that too, frigid and emotionless."

He pulled her into his arms, his cheek against her hair. "I was just so scared of my own emotions getting out of control. I never realised how much I was shutting you out."

"Don't do it again," she begged. "Never, never do it again."

"I can't promise not to feel jealousy," he said. "And you must never allow it to influence the way you live. I won't put you through the kind of hell my mother lived in for so many years."

"I know you won't. I do love you, Jethro."

"You need to say that often."

"I don't care how often I say it. But I need to hear it, too."

"You will. But there's a better place to say it."

He picked her up in his arms and strode through the open door on the way to their room. "You're going to hear it so often you'll be tired of it," he promised.

Nicola pulled his head down and brought his lips to hers as he entered the bedroom. "Never," she said with conviction as they sank down on the cover together. "Never."

READERS' COMMENTS ON SILHOUETTE ROMANCES:

"The best time of my day is when I put my children to bed at naptime and sit down to read a Silhouette Romance. Keep up the good work."

P.M.*, Allegan, MI

"I am very fond of the quality of your Silhouette Romances. They are so real. I have tried to read some of the other romances, but I always come back to Silhouette."

C.S., Mechanicsburg, PA

"I feel that Silhouette Books offer a wider choice and/or variety than any of the other romance books available."

R.R., Aberdeen, WA

"I have enjoyed reading Silhouette Romances for many years now. They are light and refreshing. You can always put yourself in the main characters' place, feeling alive and beautiful."

J.M.K., San Antonio, TX

"My boyfriend always teases me about Silhouette Books. He asks me, how's my love life and naturally I say terrific, but I tell him that there is always room for a little more romance from Silhouette."

F.N., Ontario, Canada

*names available on request

Four exciting
First Love from Silhouette
romances yours for 15 days—*free!*

These are the books that girls everywhere are reading and talking about, the most popular teen novels being published today. They're about things that matter most to young women, with stories that mirror their innermost thoughts and feelings, and characters so real they seem like friends.

To show you how special First Love from Silhouette is, we'd like to send you or your daughter four exciting books to look over for 15 days—absolutely free—as an introduction to the First Love from Silhouette Book Club℠ If you enjoy them as much as we believe you will, keep them and pay the invoice enclosed with your trial shipment. Or return them at no charge.

As a member of the Club, you will get First Love from Silhouette books regularly—delivered right to your home. Four new books every month for only $1.95 each. You'll always be among the first to get them, and you'll never miss a title. There are never any delivery charges and you're under no obligation to buy anything at any time. Plus, as a special bonus, you'll receive a *free* subscription to the First Love from Silhouette Book Club newsletter!

So don't wait. To receive your four books, fill out and mail the coupon below *today!*

First Love from Silhouette is a service mark and registered trademark.

For the woman who expects a little more out of love, get Silhouette Special Edition.

Take 4 books free—no strings attached.

If you yearn to experience more passion and pleasure in your romance reading ... to share even the most private moments of romance and sensual love between spirited heroines and their ardent lovers, then Silhouette Special Edition has everything you've been looking for.

Get 6 books each month before they are available anywhere else!

Act now and we'll send you four exciting Silhouette Special Edition romance novels. They're our gift to introduce you to our convenient home subscription service. Every month, we'll send you six new passion-filled Special Edition books. Look them over for 15 days. If you keep them, pay just $11.70 for all six. Or return them at no charge.

We'll mail your books to you *two full months before they are available* anywhere else. Plus, with every shipment, you'll receive the Silhouette Books Newsletter absolutely free. *And with Silhouette Special Edition there are never any shipping or handling charges.*

Mail the coupon today to get your four free books — and more romance than you ever bargained for.

Silhouette Special Edition is a service mark and a registered trademark.

── ── ── MAIL COUPON TODAY ── ──